STORMS OF FATE

by Harry Henig

*To my friends
Albert & Mrs. Isenberg.
With best wishes.*

H. Henig

Williams-Wallace Publishers, Inc.
Canada

Published in 1987 by
Williams-Wallace Publishers Inc.
85 King St. East
Toronto M5C 1G3

Copyright © 1987 Harry Henig

ISBN 0-88795-043-4

Published with the generous assistance of the Canada
Council and the Ontario Arts Council.
Printed and bound in Canada
Cover design: Mike Custode
Photo credit: William Johnston

Printed and bound in Canada.

PROLOGUE

There were no hills, no valleys, no rivers, and no lakes for miles around. The refugees were awed by the vastness of the flat, virgin prairie as it reached out to unite with the endless blue sky. There were a few stunted bushes and wilted poplar trees scattered about. Some came to life briefly in the summer, then dried up and withered in the fierce onslaught of winter. Winds swept south from the Arctic and with them came blizzards and paralyzing cold.

The newcomers to this strange, new land came from villages nestled among the Carpathian Mountains in Eastern Europe. Here, they faced an alien land and an alien language. But there was also hope and the opportunity for a new and better life on the broad plains of what was then the Northwest Territories of Canada, the land that in 1905 became the Province of Saskatchewan.

In the late 1880s the Young Men's Hebrew Benevolent Society was confronted with the problem of helping a vast number of Jewish refugees fleeing from the anti-Semitism of Eastern Europe. Baron Maurice de Hirsch, an international banker and philanthropist responded generously to the Society's plea for financial support. At the same time the Society successfully lobbied the Government of Canada, through John Lowe, then Minister of the Interior, for grants of homesteads northwest of Winnipeg. The settlers formed new towns, one of which was named Hirsch in honour of their first benefactor.

It was near Hirsch that Morris and Molly Finkel and their two children began a new life. The Jewish Colonization Society gave them one hundred acres of stony farmland, a three-room frame house, and some food to tide them over.

The Finkels were both born and raised in Skoronda, a

Ukrainian village in the Province of Galicia. It was a typical peasant village cradled in a deep valley, in the shadow of the ominous Carpathian Mountains. The village had survived for generations in that unknown corner of Europe.

Morris and Molly were raised in the God-affirming tradition of Chassidism. Theirs was a tradition which embraced all that was noble, honest, just, ethical and moral. These were beliefs without which life had no meaning or purpose. By believing in and communing with God through prayer, they knew they could find the courage and hope they so desperately needed to escape to a fuller, better life, where there would be no pogroms and no persecution. Their religious beliefs gave them the tenacity to endure many frustrating years.

In 1914 the Finkels were able to emigrate to the new land of hope — Canada. They arrived in a wave of settlers of both Jewish and other faiths, who took up homesteads in such communities as Sonnenfeld, Lipton, and Hirsch.

On this alien soil Morris and Molly Finkel began the back-breaking task of making a living and a home for themselves and their two boys: four-year-old Milton and one-year-old Ruben.

The Applemans and the Posareks were also new to Hirsch. Their children made fast friends with Milton and Ruben, and it was through the children that the parents could find a special bond.

His first book, *Orphan of the Storm*, is an account of his early life in Poland and on a Western Canadian farm, and his work toward eventual success in the women's retail clothing business. Of *Orphan of the Storm*, one reviewer in the *Toronto Sun* said, "It's a poignant and moving story."

"One of the most important and moving stories of our time," Lotta Dempsey, *Toronto Star*.

His second book — "*I Sold Myself a Dream* ...

"Mr. Henig has made a contribution to the history of Canadian Jewry ... it's remarkably interesting, remarkably moving and remarkably informative. It's this sort of successful writing which Harry Henig achieves in his second book."
Julius Hayman, *Jewish Standard*.

"An extraordinary autobiography by a colourful Canadian."
The book furnishes important insights not only into the man himself, but into the social history of the Canadian West as well."
Arnold Ages, Professor, University of Waterloo.

"Henig's sincerity shines like a light, it's a quality a few of the so-called professionals could use."
Connie Woodcock, *Toronto Sun*.

Elusive Summit, Harry Henig's third literary work is the biography of his daughter Sheila, a brilliant concert pianist of international fame, whose sudden death in 1979 cut short her musical career.

"Among the most special people I have ever met was the late Sheila Henig, who was one of the greatest musicians of our time. This book is therefore a tribute to her on behalf of the Canadian and international music world," wrote Maureen Forrester in the introduction.

"Brave men struggling in the storms of fate"
—Alexander Pope, 1713

CHAPTER 1

For Morris and Molly Finkel 1914 was a time for apprehension and loneliness. They were well aware that they had arrived at a destination from which there was no return. Morris laboured from dawn to dusk with pick and crowbar, digging out the rocks that were deeply embedded in the virgin ground.

The first summer passed quickly and with its passing came the icy winds from the north. Dark clouds moved in. Snow fell thick and fast, as though it were never going to stop.

"My God," exclaimed Morris to Molly one night after supper. "This is worse than the Carpathians! At least back home the huts we lived in were close together. Here we are miles away from our nearest neighbour and we're all lost in the snow. We can only hope and pray that we'll somehow survive until spring. Remember the mountain we used to climb when we were growing up?"

"Do I remember?" replied Molly. "How could I forget?"

Morris was a thin, frail man whose face was covered by a sparse, yellowish beard with brown spots on it that looked like drippings of chewing tobacco. His bulging eyes always appeared watery, as if they were about to overflow with tears at any moment. His face was the colour of clay. His beard and sidelocks were always dishevelled, as though his hair grew in different directions, and the expression on his face was frozen in time. It was hardly the face of a farmer. Yet, despite his fragile appearance, he managed to carry heavy pails of water from the well and could dig out heavy rocks when clearing patches of prairie in the summertime.

"When I was young it was a time of looking, exploring, loving," Morris continued. "Our lives were measured in small bits of experience that lodged within our memories like a beautiful horizon at sundown. For us, summer was a time for dreams and believing that they would come true, but believing always died at summer's end and reality closed in. Then came a time when things began to change, and the symphony of our childhood summers faded away. We prepared to emigrate to Canada while a door was softly but painfully closing behind us. Do you remember? Before we left, we gazed up one last time and saw the sun cast the mountain into shadows, and the birds in the green meadows played their final song for us..."

"Don't forget, we are a few years older", Molly said. "The summers you remember were made of dreams. We prayed they would come to pass before winter closed in on us. Then the believing faded away. The years have eroded our feelings. Those sights and experiences won't ever come back. The only things we have left are the memories of trees, flowers, green meadows, birds and the pearly dew at sunrise."

Molly was of medium height and very slender and she, too, was aging prematurely. Her face, though, projected the intelligence and strength of character which could endure hardship and adversity. There was also inner intensity and pride in her eyes, probably acquired by growing up in a pious Chassidic home. In the new country, however, her strength was gradually being eroded as she and her husband struggled for survival against cruel reality. She had a kind, compassionate face which often came close to smiling. She whispered continuously, as though she was praying. She was an unhappy woman.

The Finkels had been given, by the Immigration Aid Society, one horse, one cow, a few chickens and an old rusty plow. But the undernourished horse was barely able to pull the plow. Self-sufficiency was difficult to achieve.

After an endless first winter, spring arrived, to everyone's great relief, and brought with it warm, southern air on which rode soft, fluffy clouds. Everywhere warm weather beckoned and the soft breeze carried with it the sound of birds chirping on the branches of the poplar trees under an immense blue sky. Snow melted fast and sparkled as it trickled into ditches, which spread like rivulets around the farms and beyond. Fence posts were submerged gradually and resembled heads of sheep, peeping above the water.

As the years passed Morris tilled the land tenaciously, trying to survive one drought after another. At times it seemed as if the prairies would explode in flames under a merciless, scorching sun. The hard, paralyzingly long winters, which followed each short, stifling summer, were bitterly cold. The sun would set daily in a low corner of the horizon behind pink-streaked clouds and a fiery glow. Arctic shadows spread over the farms before the snow covered the prairies again.

The town of Hirsch was the focal point for miles around. It drew farmers who came to town once a week, usually on Saturday night. Hirsch's main street consisted of two small, general stores. On rainy days it appeared as if they'd grown, out of the mud that surrounded them. There was also a small, wooden shack which served as the post office. Mr. Billington, the local postmaster, sat near a potbelly stove in the winter and sat outside, swatting pesky mosquitoes, in the summer. He worked in the post office for only two hours each day, at train time. About eight o'clock in the evening the train from Winnipeg bound for the West would pull up slowly beside the small, wooden platform, stop for a few minutes, drop off some mailbags, belch heavy smoke and steam, then chug-a-lug away. In the morning, about ten o'clock, the same procedure was repeated, only in the opposite direction. No one was ever seen boarding or disembarking.

There were a couple of brown, weathered, dilapidated structures near the track, and a massive, tall, grain elevator on the opposite side. There was also a white, frame building which housed the immigrants for a few months after their arrival until a house could be built for them on their homestead.

So, there they were, Molly and Morris, liberated from tyranny and suddenly in Canada, the land of freedom and opportunity. The prairies, in the middle of nowhere, held out a vague promise of independence for them and their two boys, Milton and Ruben.

"I can't sleep," Ruben said, late one Saturday night.

"Count sheep," Milton replied, pulling the blankets closer.

"Can I sleep in your bed?"

"No. There's no room ..."

"I'm too excited to sleep — aren't you excited about tomorrow?"

"Pa only said he might let the calves out, he didn't say he would you know."

"But he must. I've already asked all my friends to come and see."

The boys had talked like that all night. As the older one, Milton pretended to be calm, but he wasn't. The day the barn door was opened to let out the calves, which were born during the winter, marked the first day of spring which, to the boys, meant a release from the confinements of the winter. Weather permitting, that day would come at sunrise.

Ruben and his brother Milton slept on a folding bed which was placed each night in the room next to the kitchen which was prestigiously called the "dining room", even though it was never used for dining. It was a warm, small room with a potbelly stove in the centre, filled with soft, damp coal that kept the fire burning slowly. The small bedroom on the left had no door; instead, there was a short, skimpy, soiled drape, hanging as a pretence to providing some privacy. Inside the room, a dark brown bed stood tightly against the wall to provide some space to get in and out of it. This was where the boys' parents slept.

Ruben got out of bed and felt his way into the dark kitchen to have a drink of water. On the way back he peeped into his parents' bedroom. He saw, by the light of the moon shining through the window, his Pa kissing his Ma. He ran back quickly to his brother.

"Milton, Milton, listen, I have something to tell you." he said, shaking his brother's shoulder.

"Leave me alone!" Milton said.

4

"No, I must tell you right now. Pa is kissing Ma!"

"What?"

"Come and see, come and see ..." Ruben insisted.

Milton couldn't resist. The boys tiptoed to the bedroom entrance and peeped in.

"Molly, please believe me," Morris said, "I love you now just as much as in Skorodna. But life here on the prairie has changed me, as it has changed everything. Are you unhappy? I am. It's my fault. It was my wish, my dream to emigrate to a democratic country and here we are, hating every minute of it."

Molly kissed him gently. "Morris, please, don't blame yourself," she whispered. "It was my wish too, to have our boys grow up in a land of freedom and equal opportunity for all. We meant well."

"What are they talking about?" Ruben asked.

"Oh, it's nothing," Milton replied. "They're sorry for coming to Canada."

"But why are they kissing each other?" Ruben wanted to know.

"It's a sort of game that grown-ups sometimes play."

"How do you know it's a game?"

"I know, Andy once told me that he had seen his parents, on many occasions, do the same thing."

"Pa could choke Ma doing that."

"Go to sleep, will you," Milty pleaded. "Everything will be fine in the morning, you'll see."

Before dawn broke, Ruben sat up in bed. The bare floor was icy cold, but he remembered his mother's warning before bedtime that "if you have an accident in bed, you'll freeze to death." He shook Milty awake.

"What?"

"I have to make you know what."

"So go, you know where the bucket is."

Ruben tiptoed into his parents' room and woke up his Ma. She knew at once what he wanted and led him into the dark kitchen.

There she held him around the waist while he used the bucket, the partial contents of which were topped with a layer of solid ice. It was not the most pleasant of necessities, but it had to be done that way because the outhouse was buried in snow and would remain that way until spring.

Despite their sleepless night, Ruben and Milton bounced into the kitchen the following morning for breakfast. Everyone, even Molly, was looking forward to some excitement which would break the monotony of a long winter. All day the boys waited with their friends, Andy Posarek and Bernie and Esther Appleman. The grown-ups seemed to be taking forever, talking and drinking tea in the kitchen. It was a warm day so the children played outside near the fenced-in pasture where the horses and cows were grazing and flicking their tails to chase the pesky mosquitoes. Flocks of birds flew overhead. Some descended for a rest on the poplar branches and chirped a phrase or two, echoing the voices of the excited children. The prairies began to pulsate with life again.

Finally, Morris and the other adults came out of the kitchen. Morris walked to the barn and opened the door. Two calves and a young, frisky colt came sprinting out, then stood still for a while as if hypnotized by the glaring sun. Suddenly they took off in all directions, jumping, running and kicking. Milton turned to his friends and boasted, as usual,

"I betcha I can run faster than any of them."

"We betcha you can't," the others replied in unison.

"I can so," he insisted.

"O.K., show us," they dared him.

He took off, lightning-fast, and within a few minutes had the colt by its tail. He hung on for a few seconds, before a hind leg came up swiftly and kicked him in the head. Milton dropped to the ground. His parents ran to him. They picked him up — he was dead.

Through the years Ruben could never understand how his parents could cope with such a tragedy. What greater sorrow could there be, even to a young mind, than to see a brother lying dead. He cried until he could cry no more and his senses became numb.

Children don't grieve for long; remembering is not for the young. Parents, however, do mourn and remember for as long as they live.

Ruben and his friends were wailing, wiping their tears with their shirt sleeves.

"Cry, cry", Mr. Appleman pleaded in a raspy voice, overcome with emotion. "Let our prayers go directly to Heaven. Collect our tears, oh God, give us strength to show us how to cope with this tragedy."

"How can I continue living when pain and anguish are clawing at my heart?" Ruben's mother lamented in Yiddish.

Although the children didn't quite comprehend what Mr. Appleman was saying, they noticed that Molly calmed down a bit. After all, it was Mr. Appleman who did the talking. He was highly respected by all who knew him for his piety and wisdom. Bernie Appleman once told his friends that his father had been blessed many years ago by a *Tzaddick*, a holy man of supernatural powers, and that was why he was so wise.

Slowly, painfully the day passed and dusk enveloped the Finkel family. The crying and the sobbing gradually subsided and the Finkels fell into a deep coma-like sleep brought on by heart-searing pain and mental exhaustion.

In the years to come, Ruben would try to block out the horrible memories, but failed. His mind would wonder back to that tragic day, and the sad weeks that followed. Even years later he would shuffle into his bedroom, sit down, press his hands against his aching head, and whisper to himself, "Why am I torturing myself with painful memories of the past? But I can't possibly forget this first, most tragic day of my life!" He attempted to divert his thoughts from the traumatic episode, but couldn't. Gradually, everything would become hazy and fade away. He would feel a sickening sensation come over him and he would give in to it and fall asleep in the hope that when he awoke, he would be rid of the tormenting vision of that fateful day.

But life had to go on, and in a few weeks activities at the farm returned to normal. Within a couple of years, Ruben grew up and was looked upon by his friends as their leader, even though he was the youngest of the group. He had a brilliant mind and was incredibly innovative. They gave him the nickname Finky, which, in their opinion, was an expression of endearment and trust. That was why, when Ruben suggested they go back and explore a pond they had come upon a few weeks earlier, they responded eagerly. At the pond they quickly undressed and plunged into the murky water, scattering the mice and gophers.

After the swim, as the boys sat on the edge of the pool, Andy, staring curiously at Finky's naked body, asked why their bodies were different from each other.

"I've never noticed any difference," said Finky.

"Let's look at them closely," Andy suggested. When they did, they were surprised to see that there really was a difference. Then Andy called to Bernie, who had wandered off. "Wow! His is the same as yours," Andy pointed out. "How come?"

"I don't know," replied Bernie. "I'll ask my Pa when I get home. He'll know. He knows everything, because he is forever reading the Bible."

He did ask his Pa that evening in order to have an explanation for his friends the following day. "My Pa said," he reported, "that Finky and I are circumcised. That's why ours are shaped differently from yours."

"What does it mean?" Andy asked.

"My Pa said that a piece of skin is cut away from the tip a few days after a Jewish male child is born."

"I guess that's the beginning of being Jewish," Finky said quietly.

"Can I be Jewish if I get circumcised?" Andy asked excitedly.

"I don't think your father would allow you to do that," Finky and Bernie replied in unison.

"I don't care what my father will say," Andy insisted. I want to be Jewish because I like Jewish food and, besides, I am going to marry Bernie's sister, Esther, when I grow up.

Bernie burst out in uncontrollable laughter. "I can just see you being a Jew. You'll look like my father, wearing a long beard and sidelocks. Oh yes! You'll also be wearing a skull-cap."

"What's wrong with that? I have seen Jews without beards," Andy defended himself. "And yet they are Jewish Jews. They even attend services in a synagogue.

"How do you know? We don't even have a synagogue."

"I know. I have seen them in Estevan when my Pa once took me there on a Saturday and, besides, some priests wear skull-caps too."

"Andy, you're crazy if you think that Esther's parents would allow her to marry you, especially a *UKe*".

Esther was sitting on a rock plucking petals off a yellow flower, and paid no attention to what she thought was a stupid conversation. Andy approached her apprehensively and asked, "Esther, don't you think I am right?"

"About what?"

"You'll marry me when we both grow up, won't you?"

"I don't like boys", she replied, without even looking up.

"I hope you'll change your mind when you get older," Andy remarked. "When I grow up," he continued, "I am going to ask you to marry me."

"Don't be so sure," Bernie interjected.

"Why not?" Andy asked, with a tinge of sarcasm.

"Because my Pa told me the other day that the time of Messiah is fast approaching. When that day comes, he said, all the mountains in the world, the oceans and the seven seas will turn upside down."

"What will cause them to do that?" asked Finky in wonderment.

"An unexpected deafening roaring earthquake will erupt

simultaneously all over the world," Bernie replied.

"How is that possible, the entire world would be destroyed?" exclaimed Finky questioningly.

"I don't know," replied his friend. "My Pa knows. He knows everything because it is written in the Holy Scriptures, I guess."

"But that's impossible," Finky insisted. "How could such a thing happen?"

To which Bernie retorted, "Don't underestimate my Pa's knowledge."

"Holy cow!" exclaimed Finky, putting his hands to his face. "If that should happen, everybody in the whole world would be walking upside down — frightening, but very funny. I wish I could be a clown when that happens," he continued wistfully. "I would make people laugh and cry at the same time. Isn't that right, Bernie?"

"I don't know," his friend replied. "I don't understand any of this ..."

Andy, who was listening to the conversation without saying a word, suddenly asked Finky, "What's a clown?"

"Haven't you ever seen one?"

"Not really."

"Well, I did," boasted Finky. "I saw one in Estevan last year. His face was painted red, he wore a funny red and yellow suit and people were laughing at the tricks he was doing. And yet, my Pa said that the clowns are very unhappy people. They make others laugh, while their own souls weep."

"Oh, forget the clowns, the Messiah, the earthquake, or whatever. Why worry about it now? We have more important things to do," Andy remarked.

"Let's go out in the pasture and try to catch some gophers," Bernie suggested. "My Pa said that he could get twenty-five cents for fifty gopher tails from Mr. Billington."

They sat in the pasture most of the summer, waiting for gophers to appear from burrows in the ground, until they

10

accumulated fifty tails, which they handed over to Bernie's father. He showed his generosity by giving each of them twenty-five cents.

Autumn was fast approaching, and those who were of school age were waiting impatiently to go to school for the very first time. It was a small, one-room, frame structure, painted red, that stood proudly in the midst of the wilted, brown grass and skimpy, scorched wheat turning golden in the August haze. Little did the children know that their lives were in the process of being reshaped while they were enjoying their simple, carefree life and freedom.

CHAPTER 2

After Milty's death, Morris became robot-like. Molly and Morris hardly ever spoke to each other and they became oblivious to Finky's existence, which made life unbearable for him. Their melancholic eyes projected constant, uninterrupted grief and there was a painful, unreal silence in the Finkel home. Words were, apparently, unnecessary between Molly and Morris; they had built up a silent communication, which no one else understood. Months passed in mute, deep dejection and fear.

When their period of mourning was completed, Morris Finkel finally decided to abandon the farm and move to Winnipeg, the big city to the east. He wrung the last tear out of Molly's heart the day he haltingly told her that soon they would have to leave the farm, say good-bye to their brown house, their unrealized dreams, and the prairies.

The sun was sinking beyond the cold horizon, and snow began falling. Night descended abruptly, and cold shadows enveloped the Prairies. The temperature hovered around forty below zero, and the farm houses were slowly being buried in snow drifts. The walls and the roofs were crackling in the grip of the paralyzing cold spell, while multicoloured reflections of the Northern Lights seeped through the heavy, snow clouds in the silence of the night, and the coyotes howled in the frozen distance.

That night, Finky's mother handed him a small bamboo case and said, "Here, pack your things right now."

"But why?" he asked.

"Because we are leaving early in the morning."

"Where are we going?"

"We are taking the train to Winnipeg," she replied, in a quavering voice.

12

"Where is Winnipeg, and what are we going to do when we get there?"

"I wish you would stop asking questions," she whispered, wiping tears off her face.

Ruben searched his father's face for some sort of explanation, but his father sat silently on a chair, staring into an ice-covered window, without any indication that he was aware of his family or the dark outside. Finky turned to his mother again and asked, "How about our cow, the horse and the chickens? We can't just leave them here to die!"

"Andy's father will look after everything," she replied.

The morning was bitterly cold and gloomy. Powdery snow was falling, piling up high against fences, blown by a blustery wind. Andy's father came over with a horse and sleigh to drive them to the train station in Hirsch. Finky suddenly had a sickening feeling in his stomach and a strange paralyzing sensation in his limbs. "So, this is it," he thought, crying quietly.

The sled slithered silently in the deep snow. Icy trees and frozen bushes rushed past and familiar fields slowly moved by. Scattered farm homes and barns buried in deep snow were hardly visible behind the banks of drifting snow. The sky was covered with low, heavy, dark clouds through which shafts of cold sunlight occasionally filtered. The snow took on a purplish hue. On the horizon, Heaven and earth appeared to be on a collision course.

Finky and his parents stood on a small, snow-covered wooden platform waiting for the train that would take them away to a strange and distant city. He saw a monstrous engine appear out of the blinding snow storm. Puffing black smoke and steam, it slowly approached the wooden shack and hissed to a halt. After a few minutes, an ear-piercing whistle split the freezing air, signalling that it was time for departure. Finky realized the full impact of the moment — the breaking-up of his world had begun. He rubbed his eyes with snow-encrusted mittens trying to quell the tears rolling down his face.

Meanwhile, his mother was attempting to board the train, carrying an orange crate containing two live chickens. The conductor refused to allow it into the passenger car. A heated argument ensued. Molly argued loudly, cursing him in Yiddish, while the conductor attempted to explain train regulations to her in English. She pushed him aside and screamed at him, her eyes glowing in anger, *"A heitug dir in bouch,* a pain to you in your stomach." After some pushing and shoving, the conductor raised his hands in surrender. Molly stuck an elbow in his stomach, squeezed past him, boarded the train, sat down on a wooden bench, and heaved a sigh of relief. The train slowly pulled away and disappeared into the raging blizzard.

"What's an anti-Semite!" she said to Finky, who edged his way in, and sat down opposite his mother.

"What an anti-Semite?" he asked her, innocently.

"One who tries to stop you from doing what you want to do, like this red-necked brute that tried to stop me from taking my two best chickens with me," she replied, while hanging on to the crate in her lap.

Later in the day, while Molly was dozing, the chickens somehow managed to get out of the crate. The commotion the frightened chickens created woke her up, and a chase began. Passengers joined in, trying to corner the frightened, fluttering birds. People jumped over benches, hats and caps flew in the air. Someone accidentally stepped on a woman's foot and she let out a blood-curdling scream. After an exhausting and chaotic few minutes, the chase was over. The chickens were cornered and put back in the crate. The passengers, perspiring and panting, settled down in their seats again.

The conductor walked over to Molly, looked her in the eye and warned her, "If you let these chickens loose again, I'll throw you off the train."

She made a fist, ready to punch him, but instead she turned to Finky and said, "You see, I told you he is an anti-Semite."

The snow continued as the train cut through a white blanket,

14

its light piercing the night and gleaming off the silver rails.

"When will we get to Winnipeg?" Finky asked.

"By midnight I hope."

"Feels like we've been travelling for weeks." Finky complained and curled up on the bench to sleep.

They arrived in Winnipeg late that night. A tall, rather tired-looking man approached them.

"I'm Mr. Berger," he said, "I'm from the Immigration Aid Society. I'll help you get settled here in Winnipeg."

He led them by streetcar to a dingy, two-room apartment above a grocery store on Andrews Street. The one window facing the street was covered with a thick layer of ice. The rooms were dark, each dimly lit from a light suspended from the ceiling. It cast a yellow colour on the grey walls.

The following day Mr. Berger returned with the good news that he had found a job for Morris at a button factory as a button-hole maker. Morris said nothing. He just followed Mr. Berger down the stairs to the street like an obedient child.

Two days later, Finky started school, but he was very unhappy.

"I miss my friends," he told his mother.

"Forget them. Forget the farm. Forget everything."

Time passed slowly for Finky at the Hebrew school, he just couldn't adjust to the strange environment and the lifestyle of the city. So, he remained a loner.

"Ma," he said, "this school or any other is not going to change anything for me. I hate it here. I feel like a stranger. I don't belong."

"We all have to try to forget Hirsch," she said sympathetically. "We are here and there's no changing that. We have to adjust, stop fantasizing. We have no alternative, complaining will change nothing. Believe me."

"I'm going to leave as soon as I can." Finky said.

"And where do you think you'll go?"

"Anywhere the train will take me. I don't care, I'll go

anywhere, anywhere to get away. Maybe to Hirsch."

"And what will that accomplish?"

"It'll get me away from father. He doesn't even know I exist."

"It's not entirely his fault. The farm was a terrible disappointment for him. And you know he blames himself for Milty's death ..."

"He cares so much for death, he's forgotten the living."

Molly sighed deeply and started to sob in her apron. Finky felt he wanted to embrace her, but he resisted that temptation, thinking it would blunt his determination to leave home forever. He suddenly realized how powerful was his need to see the world.

Winnipeg was an important railway centre, the distribution point for all of Canada to the West and the North. The railway yards were huge, especially to a homesick prairie boy, and the movement of freight trains through the intricate network of tracks was fascinating for him to watch. Even on rainy days, Ruben rushed from school to the Salter Bridge and watched fascinated as the freight trains rumbled by. The hissing of the locomotives and screeching of the wheels were music to his ears. He would close his eyes and day-dream. He had visions of distant cities and foreign countries which he hoped to visit one day but had no one to share his dreams with or confide in.

The exodus from Saskatchewan was gaining momentum and farmers were abandoning their homesteads. Many Jewish, Ukrainian and Polish newcomers could no longer continue to cope with the drought, grasshoppers, and the unbearably cold winters. Winnipeg had become the centre where they hoped to make another start for themselves.

Most of the synagogues and the Jewish schools in the north end of Winnipeg were within walking distance, regardless of where one lived. The Talmud Torah (school for study of Jewish law), located on Charles Street, and the Peretz School on Aberdeen Avenue were the focal centres of Jewish culture.

Ruben never forgot his father's walk to the ritual bathhouse on

Dufferin Avenue every Friday afternoon. On his return home, Molly served her husband a glass of tea. Then, slipping into his Sabbath robe, he would sit down and recite the *Song of Songs*. Sometimes he would sigh deeply and say, to no one in particular and in varying forms:

"This is the day of the week when my spirit rises and I feel that I am swallowed up by Divinity. Unfortunately, it only happens once a week. I like walking to the Synagogue on Friday evening and Saturday morning because by Monday the world is polluted again with vanity, hate, and greed."

Then Molly would silently recite the benedictions over the lighted candles in the brass candlesticks.

Morris, joined by other Jews in the neighbourhood who were members of the same house of worship, walked slowly to their Synagogue to perform the welcoming of the Sabbath.

They were not alone. There were many others united in worshipping God. At a long table, men sat with their heads bowed and fervently prayed, not for worldly possessions, but for the coming of the Messiah, when all evil and injustice in the world would cease. This was the place for a pious Jew, especially for Finky's father, who had severed all connections with the world since Milty was killed. He had become bitter, apathetic and terribly dejected. Only the Sabbath brought some comfort to his shattered soul; nothing else mattered any more. On such occasions Finky's childish feelings were deeply touched, and he would sometimes join the men, not from religious motivation, but rather out of curiosity.

It would take a poet to describe the overwhelming sanctity that prevailed on the approach of the Sabbath. Poor, insignificant peddlers, pressers, finishers or buttonhole makers were transformed into "angelic saints" upon entering the holy silence of the Synagogue. To them it was more than piety and a house of prayer. They seemed to feel the weight of history, and the obligation to discuss matters of Talmudic content, and miraculous stories about past generations — stories about famous rabbis, sages, prophets and holy men, their ancestors, and Jewish problems in general. They would be infused with saintliness, visualizing Heaven, and angels seated around a golden throne.

The Synagogue apparently motivated them to engage in such discussions, which could only have taken place on the Sabbath, the day of rest, when all other daily problems were swept aside until Sunday. Finky once glanced at his father during Friday evening prayers and was surprised to notice that his face, in rapturous delight, was radiant. A smile of contentment crossed his lips, he looked different on this day of the week. To Finky it was a hypnotic experience; he had never witnessed such intense, devoted piety when they had lived on the farm, but, of course, there was no house of worship there.

He profoundly believed that, had his father given him a bit of affection during his childhood, perhaps destiny would have led him in another direction, but then, maybe it was not entirely his father's fault. He struggled on the farm, forever scraping bits of nothing in order for them to survive. He had been most unhappy ever since they had arrived in Canada. Since the family had moved to Winnipeg his true happiness came only once a week on Friday at sundown. Unfortunately, Morris experienced very few Sabbaths. He died on a blustery cold day at the first onslaught of winter, when a blinding snow storm paralyzed the city. To Molly it was a devastating blow. She was destitute, helpless, lost in her limited world and worrying about Finky's upcoming *Bar Mitzvah*. She had a feeling that the sky was about to cave in on her and crush her out of existence.

In the Synagogue people gathered, candles burned, flickering in the breeze that came through the door and windows. The air was filled with unbearable silence as if the congregation was waiting for something unusual to happen. Suddenly excitement erupted, voices filled all corners and rose to a climax. The sexton's hoarse voice squeezed through the hubbub, announcing the arrival of the Rabbi. Abruptly, the noise ceased. Everybody turned towards the door, waiting for the Rabbi to enter. For young Finky, it was too painful. He just couldn't cope with so much sadness. He panicked, and ran out of the Synagogue before the funeral services began.

For Finky the period after his father's death were a most difficult time. His *Bar Mitzvah* was only eight months away. He attended special Hebrew classes in preparation for that most important day in the life of a Jewish boy — the day when he would pass into manhood. Through this period Finky was bitter and confused. He could not shake from his memory his father's last days and he was not helped by his mother's insistence that every Saturday he recite in the Synagogue, in the presence of a hushed congregation, a prayer in the memory of his father. Many times he felt like running out in the middle of the services but he nevertheless forced himself to endure it for one full year.

As a result of that, he developed an aversion to Hebrew learning institutions in general. He was, however, compelled to continue with the necessary preparation for his *Bar Mitzvah*.

Day after day, time and weather permitting, he would sit on the bridge in silent contemplation and daydreams of success would unfold in his mind's eye. He saw himself visiting many places across Canada, all the way to Vancouver and, in the end, he found himself in Stockholm. He remembered once reading a fascinating story about Sweden and he always hoped to visit that country some day.

The Salter Bridge in Winnipeg spans the entire Canadian Pacific Railway yards, where countless tracks branch out across a wide area, gleaming brightly in the summer sun. They held Finky spellbound for hours as he watched freight trains slowly crawling along and gradually slithering away from view. To him it was a mesmerizing experience — seeing yard guards chasing drifters out of box cars or from roof tops — which only increased his yearning to see the world.

One day Finky was walking out of the door when his mother suddenly screamed, "Where are you going now — to sit on the bridge, I suppose?"

"Ma," he pleaded, "I have no friends, nothing to do, what's wrong with sitting on the bridge?"

"You'll probably soon run away from home," she shouted.

He slammed the door behind him and thought, "How does she know what I'm going to do?"

She ran out after him. "Why are you torturing me?" she pleaded.

"I don't mean to, Ma, but I can't bear your crying any longer, I can't bear the stinking dark attic, and everything in general. I am trying to stay out of your way."

He was determined to hop a train just as soon as he was mentally ready. Although he knew inside that his unsophisticated background was no match for his ambitions, he also knew there was no harm in dreaming. It made life easier on the soul. It was only a matter of time before he was ready to leave home forever and escape to freedom.

CHAPTER 3

Early one Sunday afternoon, when the sun was shining and the trains were moving slowly up and down the tracks, Finky sat on the edge of the Salter bridge, studying the guards, positions and movements. He had to outsmart them in order to jump train. The engines belched thick smoke, which drifted across the bridge and obscured his view. He heard footsteps behind him. Turning, he could see through the mist of smoke the outline of a small figure. For a split second a thought flashed through his mind: "Maybe it's one of my friends, Andy or Bernie? No, that's stupid", he sadly dismissed the possibility.

He stood up, waiting for the figure to come closer. Suddenly the world began spinning. He was standing face to face with his friend Andy. In only a few seconds the unexpected, the impossible, happened. They fell into each other's arms and wept silently.

"Finky," Andy mumbled, choking with emotion.

"Andy, my buddy," Finky murmured, "this is impossible."

"No, this is a miracle," Andy replied. "It's an act of God."

"Oh, am I happy!" they exclaimed together.

"Andy, what are you doing here? When and how did you get to Winnipeg?"

Andy pointed to the curb and said, "Let's sit down a minute before we both fall over. Now, how did I get here? My parents gave up the farm, as many others did, and came to Winnipeg only a few weeks ago. We live on Charles Street, a block away from the Hebrew School."

"Boy, oh boy", Finky interjected, "I thought I would never see you again! What a wonderful day this has turned out to be! I had a premonition that something dramatic would happen to me today, but this is incredible. Let me hold your hand to convince myself that you're real."

Andy took his friend's hand and said, "Let's go to my house. My folks will be overjoyed to see you again."

On the way Finky told his friend that his father had passed away and his mother, still grieving, continued to mourn for him. "She misses him very much, even though they hardly spoke to one another when he was alive."

Whey they got to Andy's place, Yurko Posarek could not believe his eyes. "My, oh my, how you grow up!" he said in his broken English "Where you live?"

"On Andrews Street," Finky replied, happily eating cookies which Andy's mother gave him.

"I go see your mother tomorrow," Andy's father said.

"Please do, Mr. Posarek, my Ma will be very happy to see you again."

Yurko Posarek was a husky, broad-shouldered, good-natured man. He had worked in the coal mines of Boryslaw in Poland before emigrating to Canada. He was accustomed to hard work and very much enjoyed being a farmer. It offered him, for the first time in his life, a chance to breathe fresh air in a wide open world, even though the scorching sun and lack of rain dried up whatever was planted. He, like other newcomers, toiled on the land, and like so many others, the land defeated him. His wife Anna was a heavy-set woman, with a ruddy complexion and large brown eyes. They were Ukrainians, who hung tenaciously onto the culture and traditions of their ancestors.

"You know, Andy," Finky remarked, "I get very sad when I think of the open prairies we left behind, don't you?"

"Not just yet," replied Andy, "I have only lived here a few weeks."

"I miss the sunny summer days on the farm," Finky continued. "Even though grown-ups claimed that, on the farm, summer began in the middle of June and ended in September, for us kids summer never really ended. It just slowly faded into autumn which was always a sad time of year. Summer didn't really end until snow began falling."

The two boys became inseparable and were together every possible moment they could manage of each day. Finky reluctantly continued to attend special Hebrew classes, at which his friend was always present. Andy now believed more than ever that his childhood dream would some day become a reality and he would marry his sweetheart, Esther, when they both grew up.

Kildonan Park was alive with people that summer, especially on sun-drenched weekends. One Sunday Finky and Andy were sitting in the shade of a tree, reminiscing about the years they had been separated. They noticed a boy walking towards the river bank. Finky grabbed his friend's arm as if he were about to attack him, screamed, and pointed with his finger, "Look, Andy look, there's Bernie!"

"You must be nuts," his friend replied. "How is that possible?"

"It seemed impossible that we would meet, but we did", he said. "Let's catch up with him before he gets lost in the crowd."

After a short chase they caught up with him and, for a few moments, stood speechless, staring at each other. Finky was right — it was Bernie. Then all emotions broke loose. The three friends were miraculously reunited.

Bernie's parents, like many other homesteaders who had hoped to build a new life in Canada, had crumbled under the pressure of adversity. Forced to make a change, they too moved to Winnipeg. Mr. Appleman, having had years of Talmudic education, was authorized by an orthodox Rabbi to become a *schochet*, a slaughterer of animals according to Kosher requirements. They lived upstairs on Flora Avenue, trying to adjust to a strange and difficult life.

They were pious Jews who brought their religion and culture to be transplanted and preserved in the new land. Mr. Appleman was a grandson of a famous Chassidic Rabbi. His wife, Goldie, was also brought up in an orthodox home. They were known as

23

Chassidic fanatics, infused with what they believed to be "a divine spirit" that could help them perform extraordinary deeds in time of emergency, and they believed that prayer would ultimately solve their problems. Such powers were held in reserve to be used only when absolutely necessary. Although they never put them to a test, they were convinced it would work.

Together the three boys became more courageous and began exploring other parks and public places, meeting girls who would willingly indulge in necking or innocent love-making. They found out it was enjoyable but never dared to go all the way because that was considered immoral.

The Sabbath of Finky's *Bar Mitzvah* had finally come. He walked into the Synagogue accompanied by his mother, Bernie and his parents and, of course, Andy. Finky was on the threshold of assuming the responsibilities of an adult. Through the ritual, he would become a "man of duty", committed to the life-long religious and ethical obligations of his people. Finky was called up to the *Torah* to read a section in the Holy Scrolls, which he had studied for months. He was visibly nervous and apprehensive. His face was flushed, his voice raspy and quavering. It was obvious that he realized more deeply than ever before how emotionally devastating it was to be fatherless on an important event such as this. He glanced sideways and saw Andy smiling at him, nodding his head encouragingly, while his mother was sitting on a bench behind him, crying uncontrollably.

When the ceremony was finally over, he slipped out of the Synagogue, his face dripping with perspiration. Andy followed him to a prearranged meeting place. After a few minutes of silence, Finky, looking down, asked, "I was lousy, wasn't I?"

"Well, let's just say that you were better at the last rehearsal," his friend replied.

"Sooner or later everyone rises to their level of incompetence when put to a test, and today was my turn."

"There is really no reason for you to be so upset. You made it through and it's over," said Andy, trying to console him.

"Oh yes, there is," Finky replied. "I read the other day *that devastating tragedies can only create in us a ripple of sadness at the time they happen.* We are too numb to absorb the full impact. With the passage of time, however, it reaches our consciousness without mercy, for true grief seems to come in a delayed reaction!"

"You talk like a grown-up," Andy remarked.

"I am. I've been feeling old for some time now," his friend replied. "Did you hear my mother crying?"

"Yes, I did. So what?" Andy dismissed his question.

"Why do I get so upset when I hear her cry?" Finky speculated. "Is it because I am feeling sorry for her, even though I know I shouldn't? She hardly ever speaks to me and her silent treatment is making me feel guilty, as if I were responsible for everything that has happened to us, you know what I mean?" Finky paused and then continued, "My friend, I want you to know that I am very grateful to you. You understand me with your heart without my having to spell it out to you. How could I have coped with this without you?"

"Please don't thank me," Andy interjected. "I am glad to be here and with you. What are friends for, if not to help one another?"

On the Monday after the Bar Mitzvah, workmen came to patch up the leaky roof of the Jewish school. A large metal bucket with a fire burning underneath it to keep the tar hot stood near the entrance. The old teacher, who had a long beard, rested his head on his desk, dozing. Finky couldn't resist the temptation to do something crazy. He filled a dishpan with tar and poured it on the teacher's beard that was spread out like a broom on the desk. He and his friends sat quietly for a while waiting for the tar to harden, then picked up a chair and dropped it on the floor. The teacher, startled by the sudden crash, raised his head quickly. To his horror, his beard stuck to the desk top.

"You hoodlums, you bastards, you S.O.B.'s," he shouted. "You're going to pay for this," he screamed. The whole class was convulsed with laughter.

The teacher, in his late sixties, was ill most of the time. You could tell that by just looking at him. It was particularly noticeable when the snow was deep, and a freezing wind was howling. His eyes would start watering and dark blue circles would form around them. He was in constant pain from an ulcer, complaining that his mouth was very dry, but refusing to take a drink of water. He belched frequently, emitting foul-smelling gas.

The following day, he took revenge on the "young hoodlums", as he called them. He gathered them all into a small room, pretending that he had something important to announce. All eyes were focussed on him, waiting impatiently to hear what he had to say. He swiftly picked up a pail full of water and in one motion drenched them all. "Here," he said "this is my final act of reckoning. I presume you'll be glad to know that I am resigning. I'll probably never see you again, since I am leaving town tomorrow."

"Although I am sorry to see the old fart go," Finky remarked, "there is one consolation — we'll have a lot of free time on our hands with no teacher and no school. We'll have more time for other things which are more important to me than this stupid place."

The boys took off and raced home. When they got to their block Finky stopped and said:

"Look Andy, there's Mr. Silver."

"Bet you he's on his way to see Mrs. Klinger — let's follow him."

An elderly man living on the block, Mr. Silver was a widower. But, despite his age, his beer-barrel stomach and the long gray skimpy beard attached to his round fat face, he pursued Mrs. Klinger, a widow who looked quite old and was living two doors along from him. He was forever proposing to her. He was a determined realist, he claimed and once he formulated an idea in his mind he refused to give up. He had decided some months ago to marry Mrs. Klinger, pursue her, propose to her, impress her with his love for her, and make her realize how wonderful it would be for both of them if she would agree to marry him. The boys peeped through the living room window.

Mr. Silver sat with Mrs. Klinger in her living room for a long time neither one saying anything. Suddenly he reached over and tried to embrace her. She resisted and slapped his face.

"Mine dear Bessie," pleaded Mr. Silver. "If I told you once, I told you a thousand times, 'I luv you'. Tell me that you luv me too!" He looked into her watery eyes and smiled. "Nu? Say something".

But Mrs. Klinger did not respond. Bessie's fat face folded into a grin and she dared him in a challenging tone, "I betcha you couldn't perform if you tried. I betcha you don't even need a wife," she continued teasingly.

"No mine dear, you are wrong," Mr. Silver defended himself. "Give me a chance and I'll prove it to you." He took her hand gently and placed it on his lap.

Bessie reciprocated by embracing him and caressing his face. "Oi, are you a *yold*," she mumbled. "You just might still be able to do justitz to a wife after all."

"Trust me, mine dear Bessie", he pleaded.

She remained sitting still for a while, as if she were sizing him up, and finally said: "You'll have to prove yourself before I say yes or no."

"Why? Do you have someone else who is better?" he asked.

"No, silly. Motel, the coat operator, is the only von. He vonce asked me to marry him, but he is such a *shlimazel*." She waved her hand in disgust, seemingly bored by the conversation. A yawn forced her mouth wide open, exposing her loose yellow dentures. She slowly closed her jaws squeezing her teeth into place, and her face fell back to its original folds.

"Oh, forget Motel," Mr. Silver pleaded. "He chases after women. He doesn't even know why and, when he does catch von, he doesn't know what to do with her. He is almost senile."

"What does it mean?" she asked.

"It means that a man Motel's age becomes forgetful. Senility comes in two stages to a man. The first stage is forgetting to close his zipper and the second is forgetting to open it."

Bessie didn't laugh at the joke, as he expected; she obviously didn't understand it. After a few moments she asked, "How do you know such words? Is that English?"

"It must be," he replied. "My English friend told it to me." He paused, then continued, "Dear Bessie, please be mine. I am a rich man, I'll give you all the comforts and pleasures of life. Look at that beautiful house," pointing his finger across the street. "It's mine. It's all paid for. It must be worth two thousand dollars. It'll be yours. All you have to do is marry me. The painters, the carpenters and the plumbers are there, working to make it nice and clean for you."

"Big deal," Bessie replied, raising her thin grayish eyebrows. "My sister-in-law, Miriam, and her husband, Jack, live in a penty-partment donton, and you think you are Santy Clos? I am not jelis. I just want to remin you that you're not such a bagain."

"Listen to me, Bessie. I am for you, you're for me. I know you're a very good cook."

"Oh, you remember?" she asked.

"Yes, I remember, how could I ever forget your *kreplach*?"

"How about the *mitlef*, you didn't like it?"

"Oh yes, do I remember the *mitlef*! It was the night when I got terrible paints in my stomach. I was sick for a week."

"By the way, Mr. Silver, what's your first name?"

"My name is Sam."

"O.K., Sam. Give me one good reason why I should marry you? Young, you are not. Good looking you are also not. Sex you don't need, you said so yourself. So go ahead, tell me."

"Only on occasion," Mr. Silver defended himself.

"You know vat, Sam? I am not crazy about sex myself. Every time I am about to give you a treat I get a big headache. God is punishing me for just thinking about it."

"Don't worry mine dear," Mr. Silver tried to comfort her. "I feel the same way. You remember the time we almost made it? I suddenly got a splitting headache and had to give up."

"You know, Sam, we are two of a kind, we'll take a couple of aspirins before we try it again."

Sam persevered and Bessie finally yielded to his demands. He embraced her, pressed his face tightly against her oversized bosom, and whispered, "Shall we take some aspirins now?".

"Yes, why not," she agreed. "We are only old vonce!"

"You know, Bessie, there is snow on my roof but there is also fire in my furnace."

They stood up and disappeared.

"Andy, raise a white flag! She surrendered!" Finky yelled excitedly.

A few days later, Bessie and Sam were walking hand in hand down Main Street. "Mazel Tov!" They were married.

The episode of the two lovers made Finky think a lot about sex. He would be willing to try it if an opportunity would present itself, he once confided to Andy.

"Don't be stupid. Don't even entertain such sinful thoughts!" his friend warned him.

"How do you know it's sinful?"

"Because I once discussed the subject with Bernie. He told me that his father had given him a lecture on sex some time ago and, among other things, he also said, 'Wait until you grow up. Fall in love with a nice Jewish girl, get married, and then you'll have the best of both worlds.'"

"How do you fall in love?" Finky wondered aloud.

"I don't really know. I guess his father didn't tell him that."

"I think people are entitled to look for pleasures — and sex is one of them", Finky said. "You must feel important and self-confident when you fall in love. You see, I feel that in order to get on in this world you have to have *chutzpah*, you have to be determined. The more confidence you have in yourself, the more likely you'll make your dreams come true."

"But don't you know", asked Andy, "that what you might call success can be destructive to a person who's too young and doesn't know yet how to handle it?"

"Of course I'm aware of that", responded Finky. "But remember, when you achieve something, when you win prestige or respect, every time you do, you get a bit wiser. I remember hearing somewhere that 'a winner never quits and a quitter never wins.' You see, it can be a vicious circle. When you have an idea, or a dream, on your mind all the time, you must pursue it hard and never give up if you're hoping to get results, if you're going to win."

"You sound as if you have something specific in mind," said Andy.

"I do", Finky replied. "I've lived with one particular dream for years. Now I feel the time is fast approaching when I'll say good-bye to you all, spread my wings, and fly away."

Finky gestured with his hands as though he had wings and continued, while Andy sat entranced.

"I have a feeling that destiny will lead me in the right direction and then I'll be able to explore the meaning of life, and perhaps even find some happiness. Andy, in case I don't see you again before I take off, I want you to promise me that you will pursue your dream, you will see Esther as much as possible, and try to make her see things your way. Remember Mr. Silver! He didn't give up."

"I've no intention of giving Esther up," Andy assured his friend. He then turned back to Finky's plans. "Will you tell your mother that you're leaving?" Andy asked.

"I don't think so," Finky replied. "She doesn't seem to care what I do. She may be better off without me. Say good-bye to Bernie and Esther for me, just in case I don't see them before I go."

The two boys embraced each other for a brief moment, then each went his own way, without looking back. On his way home, Finky had further thoughts about the future:

"There must be more to living than horsing around with girls — that's not the answer to my ambitions. It's a big world, and I'm going to find out what it's all about. I'm sorry to leave Andy and Bernie behind after all the time we've been apart and then so recently come together again. But perhaps some day our paths will cross — it happened once and it could happen again. It looks as though life is full of mysteries and miracles. I just have to find mine."

Finky tossed and turned in his bed all night, then recalled a passage he had come across in the *Saturday Evening Post*.

"Youth is a time for exploring and believing; youth is courage, audacity, and clear blue skies, even on cloudy days. Youth is yearning, reaching out to places where neither of us has ever been."

He pondered upon the words, then snuggled down to sleep.

"I think I'm as ready as I'll ever be," he thought. "The possibilities for the future look endless to me and they are certainly intriguing. I know my background is humble and it hardly matches my ambitions, but I'm certainly going to explore. Perhaps I'll find a different and even more satisfying life."

With such thoughts in his mind, and with a mixture of excitement, anticipation, and even some guilt, Finky's mind was made up — he was going to leave.

CHAPTER 4

The day was bright when Finky took the small bundle he had prepared the night before, and quietly walked out of the attic and down to the bridge. He descended the steps and ran towards a long freight train that was slowly crawling westward. He approached it with trepidation in his heart, not knowing what to expect on his journey of no return. He noticed an open door in one of the cars, jumped in, leaned against a wall, and listened to the sound of his heart pounding. There was no doubt in his mind that a door was closing behind him, blotting out painful memories, forever. While the locomotive was puffing and wheels were screeching, Finky realized that the streets, the houses, the green parks — everything he was leaving behind — were drenched in sunshine and gradually disappearing from view. He was also aware that to reach a new horizon he would have to face many problems. He was nevertheless hanging tenaciously on to a vision that he would be a rich man one day. Just thinking about his rendezvous with destiny triggered a shiver up and down his spine.

The rhythm of the wheels, with every turn, seemed to be saying, "Freedom, freedom, freedom." It was hypnotic and Finky fell asleep.

Suddenly, excruciating pain in his back made him scream involuntarily. He had been kicked while asleep. He looked up and saw a man in uniform standing over him.

"What in the blazes are you doing here? Don't you know that it's against the law to ride freight trains? Where are you from and what's your name?"

"I am from Winnipeg and my friends call me Finky," he replied in a shaky voice.

"I could arrest you, but I'll give you a break and allow you to clear out of here at the next stop."

The guard jumped from the car and vanished. At the next stop, Finky decided to risk arrest and stayed on the train. No guard appeared, nor did one at any later stop.

After two days and nights the train finally came to a halt. Finky jumped out, looked around and saw other drifters crawling out of hiding spots. He edged his way up to a soot-covered man and asked, "Can you tell me where we are?"

"In Regina," he replied.

"Do the guards always chase you around like this?"

"Wait, you ain't seen nothin' yet!"

After roaming around the freight yard for a while, he noticed an empty freight car, its doors open, parked on a dead-end track. Inside, a man was sitting on top of a crate drinking coffee. Finky stared at him hungrily and said, "Hi."

"You look like you crawled out of a sewer," the man remarked. "You want a coffee?"

"Do I ever! I haven't eaten since yesterday."

"Here, have this," he said, handing Finky a sandwich.

"Thanks a million."

"Where are you aiming for?"

"For Vancouver," Finky replied.

"It's going to be mighty tough getting there," the man warned him. "Now, here is some advice. Stick around the track over there," he said, pointing with a coffee pot he was holding. "A train is due to leave on that track later tonight. If you're lucky you'll sneak in unnoticed under cover of darkness." Abruptly, before Finky could say a word, he picked up his lunch-box and walked off along the endless tracks.

On the third night after Finky jumped onto a moving freight train in Regina, he opened the box car door a few inches for some fresh air. He saw blinding flashes of lightning splitting the black clouds and felt the heavy thunder shaking the ground as it reverberated against the towering mountains. Every minute the night grew heavier and darker. Intense blackness covered the valley. Rain mixed with hail soon enveloped the entire area, while the train heaved and puffed along the track. Somewhere, far away, a hoarse locomotive whistle echoed mournfully through the valley. The train slowly wormed its way out of the deep dark shadows and an endless expanse of tracks appeared. "This must be Vancouver," he thought, as the long monster gradually reduced speed and came to a halt.

Finky jumped out into a pelting rain, looked around quickly for any guards, and began running in the direction of a barely visible light in the distance. He pressed his body tightly against a dilapidated clapboard wall of a saloon, crept up to a dirty window and saw sailors, grizzled winos and a variety of dead beats. Some were slouching in semi-darkness against the bar, drinking and occasionally grabbing at the waitresses as they passed by with their trays loaded with beer. Others, at the tables, engaged in arm-wrestling or cards. There were a few further back in the corners, necking with skimpily dressed women. A tall, heavy man with a long black moustachio was sitting behind the bar, picking his nose. The aroma of beer, grease and French fries, mixed with a distinctly human, sweaty, stinking odour wafted through the broken windows.

Finky, edging closer to the window to see better, suddenly became aware of a hand touching his shoulder. He looked around. He faced a girl, who was soaking wet. She stared at him for a few seconds and asked him with surprise in her voice, "Who are you? What are you doing here on a night like this?"

"I could ask you the same question," Finky boldly replied.

"I work here," she said. "My brother Tony owns this saloon. My name is Laura."

Finky couldn't help noticing her pleasant round face and long brown hair. "I wish she would ask me to come inside," he thought.

"Where are you from?" she asked.

"I'm from Winnipeg and my friends call me Finky. I just arrived on a freight train a few minutes ago. I hope I'm in Vancouver."

"You are," she assured him.

"I never thought of this city being so dilapidated," he said uncertainly.

"This is skid row — the slums. All you'll find here are cheap restaurants, saloons, flophouses, bums, drunks and thrill seekers. Come on kid, let me get you something to eat."

"Please, don't call me 'kid'. I'm almost sixteen," he said defensively. She smiled, reached for his hand, took him inside, and said, "Sit here, I'll get you some grub." She disappeared behind a swinging door. A few minutes later she reappeared, carrying a bowl of soup and a few slices of bread, which she placed on a rickety table and then nodded to him.

"Here, eat this, you look like you haven't eaten in a month." He thanked Laura over and over, while devouring the food like a starving dog.

Late that night, it stopped raining and clouds began drifting across the sky. With every break in the clouds, the moon reappeared. Finky sat in the saloon, fascinated by the weird characters while watching the uninhibited sexual activities in progress. Tony looked at him, then turned on his sister and shouted, "Ya may be my sister, but you're a damn bitch."

"What in the hell's all that about?" Laura asked, fuming with anger.

"Tell me, when will ya stop bringing strays and free-loaders into this joint? I see ya got yourself another one. Where the hell did ya find him? Win him in a poker game?"

"You shut up your big mouth," Laura screamed, and stop acting like a big shot, just because you own this rat-infested hole. What's the matter with him anyway?" She pointed at Finky, "He's better than the usual scum you have me look for!"

"He's too young, that's what," Tony shouted back.

"I like him and intend to help him whether you like it or not! And if you don't shut up, I'm walking out of here for good! You can find yourself a pimp to procure weirdos for your lousy business!" Laura draped an old coat over her shoulders, turned to Finky, and said, "Come with me, kid. I'll find a spot for you for the night."

Tony got terribly upset over his sister's threats and began apologizing. "I'm sorry. Please, Laura, don't go! I lost my head for a minute!"

She ignored her brother, turned to Finky and said "Come on upstairs, big boy. Let me give you a hot bath. You stink like a skunk."

"Holy cow, I hope she doesn't insist on washing me. I would be terribly embarrassed if she saw me in the nude," thought Finky. He had a feeling that having sex with Laura was inevitable. "Let it happen. I've been wanting it for years. Why resist it now?"

Apprehensively, but obediently, he followed her into a dark room and sat down on a chair near a dirty window. His head was throbbing and his mouth was sand dry. He could see, although faintly, that the moon was moving closer and casting shadows on the walls. Laura moved beside him, took hold of his hands and whispered, "It's been my dream meeting someone like you."

"Why, what's so special about me?" he managed to ask.

"You're cute, young, innocent and scared. But most of all I have a sneaking suspicion that you're a virgin. Am I right?"

"Sort of, I guess," he whispered, while looking down at the floor.

"There's really nothing to be nervous about," she reassured him. "You'll see." She slowly, methodically proceeded to undress him and helped him into the tub. Although saying nothing directly about it, she was surprised by the evidence of his physical maturity.

"How old did you say you are?"

"I'm almost sixteen," he murmured, feeling excitement coming over him.

She helped him out of the tub, drying him with a rough towel. Pointing to a dark, gray bed, she said, "You'll sleep here tonight. I'll bring you up a blanket in a few minutes."

Next thing he knew, Laura was covering the two of them with a blanket as she crawled into bed, cuddled up close to him and whispered "Hold me tight!"

He slowly, hesitantly, moved his trembling hands over her soft quivering body, down her back, lower and lower to her perspiring thighs. For Finky, it was the first time he felt someone's hands caressing him so intimately. It was a thrilling, electrifying experience to which he willingly surrendered. The room was spinning ever so fast and he heard himself uncontrollably whispering, "Oh, you beautiful bundle of joy! I love you very much. Promise you'll never leave me!"

"I promise," Laura sighed deeply.

In the blinding frenzy of their passion they got lost in each other's arms and the world ceased to exist.

That night Finky lost his virginity and for the first time realized his sexual fantasies. He was also liberated from the curiosity and inhibitions that plagued him since his first awareness of love and sex. He found it to be gratifying beyond his wildest expectations, which made him begin speculating about his own beginning. But above all, he finally felt he was a man and began to understand more about life, desire and creation. He felt mentally ready for bigger things that, hopefully, would cross his path in years to come. "The beginning of a plan is very important," he thought, "if properly implemented." Laura certainly gave him a good start.

The following morning Laura served him some breakfast. Finky turned to her and asked, "Do you sometimes go to bed with those degenerates downstairs?"

"I do if they have the price," she replied.

"I thought I was an exception even though I didn't even have the price," he murmured accusingly.

"You are different. I never had sex with a virgin before." She took him by the hand and he followed her out of the saloon.

They boarded a bus that took them some distance out of town. There was a beautiful forest with tall trees reaching for the sky and grass that was luscious and green. They sat for a while, looking at one another, and felt their passion rising. Laura suddenly started running down a hill towards a country road. Finky, in pursuit, grabbed her from behind and both disappeared into the tall grass along a dusty road. Finky's adventurous mind was obsessed with a compulsive determination to achieve, to possess, and enjoy life

37

to its fullest.

The thirties were bad years. The deep depression ruined lives, dashed dreams, devastated countries, and Canada was no exception. People drifted, riding freight trains from the Atlantic to the Pacific, searching for work. Starving hordes of unemployed stood in relief lines for hours, waiting to be handed a bowl of soup. Hot winds and the scorching sun destroyed everything farmers hd toiled to create for years. Day after day Finky walked Vancouver streets, hoping to find some work but had to settle for an occasional few hours loading a freighter or driving a truck on the docks. He would offer Laura the few dollars he earned. She always refused to accept it, and never failed to give him some food.

Finky, walking the streets one day in search of work, came upon a block of garages, car parts stores, repair shops and auto wrecking companies. In front, there was a line-up of men, looking as if they were expecting something to be handed to them. After standing in line for over an hour he finally reached a booth. Inside there was a man stripped to the waist, screaming "Move it, move it!"

"What's going on here?" he asked.

A fat perspiring face appeared in the open wicket and demanded, "What d'ya want?"

"I understand you are hiring."

"So what?"

"Is the job still available?"

"It sure is," the man replied. "Those guys want money but refuse to earn it." He pointed with his fat dirty hand. "Are you hungry?"

"Very," Finky replied.

"The company needs a strong boy to wash old car parts in gasoline — motors, axles, transmissions — everything that could be resold to garages."

"Where do you get the parts?"

"From the backyard, stupid! We wreck cars here at the back, bring the parts inside, have them washed and sell them. You want

38

to take a crack at it?"

"Sure, why not?" Finky replied.

"The hours are from 8 a.m. to 6 p.m. The pay is three dollars a week. See you in the morning!" He slammed the window shut.

Walking back to convey the good news to Laura, Finky was obsessed with a feeling of satisfaction. He was proud of his achievement. "Never give up," he murmured to himself. "Keep on trying until you succeed. Persistence pays off."

A week later, Finky was still at the rear of the store, wearing a heavy dark blue apron and standing over a deep metal sink filled with gasoline. The room was loaded with greasy, oil-encrusted auto parts, which he soaked in gasoline and scrubbed with a wire brush.

He was pale, listless and slightly dizzy. The skin on his hands had shrivelled from the powerful cleaning fluid. The fumes were gradually making him ill, but he was determined to hang on. One day, he stumbled out to the front of the store, and collapsed. An ambulance was called and he was rushed to the hospital. The attending doctor reported that he had been overcome by gasoline fumes and released him. He returned to Laura, who nursed him back to health.

CHAPTER 5

Finky stayed with Laura but, over the span of a few years, his self-confidence eroded to its lowest level. Fame and fortune escaped him and that made him wallow in self-pity. He remembered a co-worker saying to him once: "If you believe that you will meet with success in this country, forget it! You are in the wrong place! Go abroad, to Spain, Japan, or even Sweden. I hear that opportunities in those countries are endless."

"Perhaps the man is right," Finky thought. "I have wasted close to five years in this part of the country doing odd jobs on the waterfront. I have tried to learn the car business for three dollars a week, and got ten cents an hour for overtime if I was lucky. Next month is my birthday. I'l be twenty-one years old. How fast time has flown. I guess I'm no different from others. We are all striving for a better life, chasing a dream. We stumble along blindly until our spirit gives out. Some would continue their struggle and grab whatever comes their way. Such individuals are 'men of all trades, and masters of none' or rather they have a talent for everything except success."

His mind ill at ease, as it so often was, Finky wandered along Georgia Street until he found himself near the entrance to Stanley Park, a thousand acres of natural forest, sandy beaches, gardens, a zoo, an aquarium, a vast domain for play or rest. Unable to make up his mind whether he should join the throngs of pleasure seekers, he leaned against a tree and watched idly as traffic passed through the gates.

A long, gleaming limousine drew up to the curb, a short distance away. A uniformed chauffeur jumped out, ran around the car, and opened the rear door. From the Rolls stepped a tall, slim, beautifully-dressed woman. Her pale blue dress matched her sparkling eyes. Her long blonde hair shone in the warm sun. Finky heard her say to the chauffeur, "Thank you, Pierre."

"What a name for a chauffeur!" thought Finky. "If I ever get rich, I'd want a car like that and a 'Pierre' to drive me around. That's class!"

Suddenly, as though out of nowhere, an ill-dressed figure appeared, snatched the purse from the woman's hand, and dashed down Georgia Street. The woman screamed. Several passers-by gave chase. One of the pursuers was Finky. Half a block away Finky overtook the thief, grabbed him by the waist and pulled him to the ground. The older but much bigger and huskier man punched Finky and dazed him. Finky lost his grip. The thief jumped to his feet and took off, leaving the handbag behind. Finky picked it up. Rubbing his jaw, he made his way back to the park entrance.

The woman rushed forward and threw her arms around him.

"Thank you, thank you so much!" she cried out. "You're a brave young man. You really shouldn't have done it — why, you might have been killed. But I am so glad to have my purse back. It's not the money in it so much as the papers, and the cards and photos that can be so hard to replace if they're lost. Thank you so much. I hope he didn't hurt you badly."

"It was nothing", replied Finky, embarrassed by all the attention he was receiving, especially within the hearing of several bystanders standing near in idle curiosity.

The woman seemed to be in no hurry to leave.

"Now that's over — except for your sore jaw — can you tell me something about this place, because I'm a stranger here", she said. "Is that the main entrance to the park?"

"Yes, ma'am", Finky replied.

"Would you show me around a bit, if you have the time?" the woman said. "And please don't call me ma'am. It makes me feel like an old lady, and I'm not. And that you are some kind of servant, which you are not."

"I'll be glad to show you the park, but we won't be able to see it

41

all today. It's far too big for that."

The woman looked at him with her cool blue eyes, a sensuous smile on her lips.

"I hope you can show me the park another time ..., I don't know your name."

"Ruben Finkel", he stammered. "But my friends call me Finky."

"I hope I can be a friend of yours," the woman said.

"You sure can," he responded excitedly, with thoughts already in his mind of how suddenly important he had become. "In fact, I'd be delighted and proud to be your friend."

"Good, that's settled," she said. "But if we're to be good friends, you have to know my name. It's Helga, and I live in Stockholm, Sweden."

Upon hearing her brief introduction, Finky felt his hopes beginning to rise; he just might be in the right place at the right time. "I must not blow this chance," he thought. "Perhaps I can turn it into a close relationship. This could be the beginning of a friendship that might turn my life around."

He felt even more sure of a possibly better future when Helga said, "I have to go, but I still want you to show me Stanley Park. Can you do this for me tomorrow?"

"Certainly, I'd be delighted," he replied eagerly.

"Good!" Helga said. "I'll drop you off at your place now and on the way we'll decide where and when to meet tomorrow. Where do you live?"

Finky hesitated — he did not want his new friend to know about Laura. "I'm temporarily staying with friends until I get myself settled. They live quite near here and I can easily walk," he said, pointing toward the mass of apartment buildings in Vancouver's West End on the eastern approaches to Stanley Park. At that moment the limousine drew up to the curb and Helga, as Pierre opened the door for her, said nothing more except, "Then I'll see you tomorrow at three, right here." With a wave of the hand she entered the car and disappeared in the traffic.

Finky, his mind in a turmoil, returned to his squalid quarters. He could not talk to anyone about what had occurred nor about his hopes, which at this time could as easily be in vain as become reality. It was, therefore, with a mixture of temerity and confidence that he made his way to the entrance to the park where yesterday he had first seen the woman who might change his destiny. Sharp at three o'clock the limousine arrived, and Helga was there as she had promised.

For the next two hours Finky was in mental paradise. There was so much to see, and Helga was interested in everything, from a display of Haida Indian totem poles to a miniature railway.

"I'd like very much for you to have dinner with me", Helga said, as the Finky-escorted tour approached its end.

"That's very kind of you, but ..." Finky responded, trying to give her the impression of uncertainty, while inwardly his heart leaped with the joy of anticipation.

"But what?" asked Helga, a little sharply.

"Nothing really, except that I'm not properly dressed for dinner."

"Nonsense! Perhaps you'd like to wear a tuxedo?" she joked. Then Helga went on: "I have something to talk to you about, an idea that might interest you, and I think we can do it best at the dinner table."

As her blue eyes excitingly looked into his, Finky hesitantly accepted the invitation and when Pierre arrived with the car he sat with his hostess in the back seat.

Dinner, more lavish than anything Finky had ever had, was served in Helga's hotel suite. Then, after she poured glasses of cognac for them, she spoke what was on her mind:

"You told me yesterday that you were staying temporarily with friends until you found a place. Now, would you like to stay with me until, as you say, you get settled?"

For a few seconds he did not know what to say. An invitation of this kind had only been in his dreams. He knew very little about Helga. During their conversations in the park that afternoon she had mentioned a few things about herself: she had been born in

Austria, her father had been a diplomat, she was a divorcée, with no family and, as she put it, much time on her hands. "I travel alone" was her brief affirmation, except for Pierre. She gave evidence of great wealth.

"Yes, of course I will", Finky replied, his voice tinged with gratitude. "I couldn't turn down such a wonderful invitation if I tried. Until now I have never believed in fate, but you have just converted me — I have become a fatalist. It must have been my destiny to go to the park, otherwise I never would have met you. I have no intention of refusing such an offer as yours."

They celebrated the occasion with more cognac, then Helga took him by the hand and led him to her bedroom. Finky's thoughts ran in one direction: "She expects me to go to bed with her and she is not wasting any time. I should have realized what she had in mind by the way she looked at me. Sex is a part of the communication that unites two people. I'll do my best to achieve that unity."

When they awoke the next morning, Helga asked, "Are you sorry about what we did last night?" He assured her he had no regrets, except for one thing, "Yes, I am sorry the night did not last for at least a week."

The next evening Finky decided not to join Helga for dinner. He did not want to make it too obvious he was interested in her. He didn't want her to think that he was an opportunist. Yet in his mind he was manipulating, trying to calculate what his next move should be. He knew that he had to impress her, but he was aware that he was not about to fall in love with her as he imagined she was expecting him to do. To Finky, for the time being at least, theirs was strictly a coincidental meeting and their feelings towards each other those of friendship which could, in time, perhaps develop into a meaningful relationship.

Helga, however, had different ideas. She had been living and travelling alone for some years, hoping that some day she would meet a man who would become a part of her life, willing to be a companion with commitments. In time that association might become a more intimate relationship that would bring happiness into each other's life. Helga, an astute business woman who had turned a rich inheritance and a substantial divorce settlement into great wealth, was a brilliant judge of character and talent. She was satisfied that Finky — bright, ambitious, and, most importantly, obviously hungry for recognition — could, with the training she could supply, become a successful entrepreneur. Finky was the one she had been looking for.

The association they established had its periods of stress. On one occasion Finky left Helga ("on business", he told her) and promised to call her within a few days. The days became weeks, and there was no call. At last the telephone rang and Helga heard his familiar voice.

"Helga my dear, how are you?"

"If you want to know how I am, why don't you come over and find out? I thought you were never going to call. Where have you been?"

"I am sorry about that, but I've been out of town and I just got back. I'll be there in about an hour."

As Finky hung up the phone, he knew that he was close to a crisis in his relationship with Helga. He had dreamed for years of something like that to happen. Now it had happened, it was real, yet he hesitated to commit himself.

That night Helga clung to him passionately, she wanted him desperately. In the early morning hours she promised to make him a partner in her enterprises in Spain and Sweden just as soon as they arrived in Madrid, which was the headquarters of her corporate operations. That would be in three to four weeks, she said.

"You have a lot of rough edges", she told Finky, "but I'll polish them up in due course."

Finky, overwhelmed by the magnitude of her promises, hoped that some of them would materialize. Many hours later, after dinner, Helga talked to Finky:

"I don't want you to get the impression that I am a manipulator. But I do want you to know that I am very fond of you and I could probably help you achieve some of your hopes and aspirations. From what you have told me about yourself, I would say that you have an inferiority complex. That can be changed into an assertive positive attitude. If you are willing to give me a few weeks, I guarantee that you'll be ready to conquer the world. What do you say?"

His voice filled with excitement, Finky cried out, "When do we start?"

"We start tomorrow", said Helga. "You will be in charge of my mail, my messages, my appointments, and other things, and you will be paid the going rate. I'll be going to Spain very soon, and you will go with me. We are going by sea and we'll have time to get to know each other better."

As Finky and Helga embraced, he suddenly felt a tinge of guilt — he remembered Laura, who had done so much for him. But the thought of Laura vanished as quickly as it came as Helga and he clung tightly to each other.

The thought of Laura became a reality the next time Finky was in Tony's saloon. He had not seen her for weeks, now he had to tell her he was leaving Vancouver. They met at the bar.

"Where in the hell have you been?" she demanded. "I've been sick worrying about you."

"Yes, it's been a long time. I just had to get away to think things out. Now I have something to tell you, and I hope you will understand."

She stared suspiciously at him.

"Laura", he said. "There is someone else in my life. She's a divorcée, and very rich. I like her. She's on a trip around the world and she wants me to go with her."

He took Laura's hands in his and continued apologetically.

"I'm truly sorry, because you've done so much for me. But I have a feeling that my destiny is about to change. This is the opportunity I've been dreaming about, and it may never come again. I must not let it pass me by. It was meant to be. Of course I'll be forever grateful for everything you've done for me. You gave me love, my first time — something I will never forget. But now I have a chance to see the world and I am really sorry that it just

46

can't include you. I know it sounds shallow but I am sure this is the beginning of my dream becoming a reality."

"I'll miss you", Laura said. "When are you leaving?"

"A week from tomorrow."

Tears down her cheeks, Laura lowered her head and murmured, "Tony was right, a stray hardly ever settles down. But, Finky, if you ever need me again, I'll be here for you." She turned away from the bar and slowly walked away. She did not look back before the door of the saloon closed behind her. Finky's eyes followed her, while his heart felt as though it was about to break. Then he got up and left the room by another door. "What a noble soul she is, she didn't even make a scene," he thought.

Laura was all but forgotten in the passion and the ecstasy of the nights with Helga. He saw Laura once more before his departure from Vancouver. As the liner was leaving the dock, Finky and Helga were on an upper deck, waving and throwing streamers to the noisy crowd on the pier. Then Finky's eyes found Laura. She was waving a white kerchief from a far corner of the pier. He blew several kisses in her direction and felt pangs of guilt as he realized that he was leaving behind a real friend who had done for him more than he had ever expected. But it was too late to do anything about it now — the liner was slowly manoeuvring its way out of the harbour, heading for the unmarked highways of the ocean.

That night the moon and stars appeared and the dusky sky merged with the water at the rim of the fascinating horizon. Helga kissed Finky on the forehead, and said, "Come on, my Don Juan, let's go below — the champagne's chilled and waiting."

In their luxury suite they sipped the champagne.

"Here we are, off together on a long ocean voyage, going to countries you have never seen, yet there is very little you really know about me."

"Just knowing you is good enough for me", said Finky, firmly.

"Thank you for saying that", said Helga. "But considering our wonderful relationship and how even closer we will be in the

47

future, you ought to know more about me than you do.

"My father was a diplomat and his name was Herman — Herman Haufer. My mother died when I was only a week old. I know almost nothing about her because my father never ceased to mourn her sudden death and would never answer any of my questions about her. So of course I was raised by nannies and nurses, and was sent to the best schools in Austria and in other countries where my father was stationed. We did a lot of travelling and during one of our tours, this time to Spain, my father introduced me to a most interesting gentleman who was also in the diplomatic service. His name was Frantz Klieger, who was of German descent, although he had been living in Stockholm for some years. He was fifteen years older than I.

"Then a terrible tragedy came upon me. My father was killed in an automobile accident on the streets of Madrid. Frantz Klieger did his best to comfort me while I stayed with other friends, trying to get over the shock I had had. Then, one evening Frantz proposed marriage and I, being terribly naive and vulnerable, accepted his offer. Just as soon as the arrangements could be made we were married.

"We lived in Madrid for the first five years of our marriage. Then Frantz was transferred to Switzerland and we spent happy years in Berne, in a mansion which my husband owned. I remember those years as possibly the happiest I have had. Then Frantz was ordered to go to Greece. I loved my home, my friends, and the city in general, and I refused to go. He moved out and left me behind. He returned to Berne from time to time to argue with me, but I wouldn't budge. Finally he wrote from Athens, asking, as he said, for the last time whether I would have a change of heart but I never replied. Throughout the years I was used to having things my own way and was not prepared to compromise.

"Since I was the only heir to my father's estate, I inherited more than I could handle. I also received a substantial amount of money and property from my husband when my marriage ended in divorce. That affected me deeply. I turned everything over to my father's lawyers in Madrid, who, within a few years, more than doubled the value of my financial investments.

"For some time I tried to ignore my loneliness and disappointment, until it turned to utter despair. To relieve my emotional state, I asked my chauffeur Pierre to accompany me on a trip around the world. I wanted to visit all those places I have never been to before in the hope of finding some peace of mind, which I so desperately needed. Intuitively, I felt all along that one day I would meet someone who would make my life worth living again. By sheer luck or coincidence, when I noticed you standing near the Stanley Park entrance in Vancouver, my heart skipped a beat and I knew I had found my liberator."

"Why are you telling me all this?" Finky protested. "It sounds like a confession. I love you for what you are, not for what you possess."

"Hush, my dear, let me finish. I want you to know that I have enough money for both of us, as well as Pierre. We can live in luxury anywhere in the world and I want to share it all with you because I love you."

"My dear Helga, I would love you just as much even if you didn't have a dime, I swear. I adore you. You are the most wonderful thing that could have ever happened to me, please believe me."

"I believe you", she replied, an unmistakable sparkle of love in her eyes. "I'm looking forward to a long and happy life and that, when the time comes, we can retire together to a place I have on Lake Malaren, outside of Stockholm. It's a beautiful villa, near the beach, where we can — and will — enjoy life to the full."

Once they were in Madrid, Finky discovered that Helga had many friends, some of whom eagerly helped her settle in a house she owned there. It was a luxurious mansion, of the kind that Finky had never seen before, except in home fashion magazines or the movies.

Finky quickly settled into the enjoyment and serenity of his new life. Not all of his days were occupied only with pleasure. He spent long hours studying the running of Helga's financial and business affairs under her tutelage and that of the trustees who managed things in her absence. The hours of study and of managerial work were long and often arduous and trying. But he was determined to learn, so that he could rightfully share in the investments she had promised to him in Canada.

Four years passed quickly for Finky who was immersed in work, slowly for Helga. She began to show signs of boredom and restlessness. It was then that she decided they should take a cruise. She and Finky invited several close friends to accompany them and they took Pierre with them as the essential factotum. Finky, at first reluctant to leave his work, found relaxation such as he had never had before. For him, stretched out in the sun, his beloved beside him, on a luxury yacht on the velvet waters of the Mediterranean, life was good. By now he felt sure that his dream had come true.

CHAPTER 6

Back in Canada, winter was slowly ending. It was the end of April and in Winnipeg it seemed that spring had finally arrived. Andy, in deep contemplation, sat on a bench in Kildonan Park. He wondered what more he could do to prove to Esther's parents that he loved their daughter. He heard footsteps behind him.

"How did you know I would be here?" he asked.

"You said last night you had some serious thinking to do today, so I took a calculated guess that I would find you here."

She was tall, slender, had a face of an angel, and penetrating, trusting blue eyes. He took her hands, looked into her eyes, and asked, "Have I ever told you how much I love you?" He swept her into his arms and pleaded, "Tell me that you love me as much as I love you."

"I do, I do," she replied, "forever and ever. Otherwise I wouldn't have come. Nothing in this world will keep us apart, I promise! How about you?"

"When I think of you, which is always, I hear birds singing and dazzling butterflies are whispering your name!" Andy replied.

"Does your father know about us meeting like this?" Andy asked suddenly.

"No, he doesn't. We must tell him soon."

"You know, of course, that our lives depend on our love for each other," Andy continued. "It has been my dream ever since we were children on the farm that we would be united one day."

"Yes, I know," she whispered, "I remember".

Although the park was crowded, the two lovers were totally oblivious to everything. The water of the swollen Red River was galloping and cascading over and under the natural ice sculptures created by the spring thaw. Orchid buds, tiger striped cups and lavender crowns were being reborn in the spring sunshine. The breezes were refreshing and warm and the nearly nude trees were beginning to bloom while the grass below turned soft and green. Andy and Esther sat holding hands in silence under a huge tree and watched rain drops falling from a sudden spring shower.

Andy looked into Esther's eyes and asked, "Have I ever told you how beautiful you are?"

"Only a thousand or more times," she replied. "I stopped counting after that."

"I'm extremely happy that I have persisted through the years. I never for a moment gave up hope. All there is left for us to do is to approach your parents with determination and wish for the best".

The brightness of the spring day gave way to a dark, wind-swept evening. A sharp gust of wind caught the edge of a loose shingle in the roof above the Appleman attic, creating a whistling sound that reverberated through the ceiling. Andy and the Appleman family gathered in the kitchen, the largest room in the attic where Andy pleaded his case.

"I never for one minute stopped hoping that this day would come, even though you tried through the years to discourage me in every way possible and to reject me completely. But Esther has always come to my rescue, reassuring me, asking me not to give up. I identify with Jewish people. I want to be Jewish. I am willing to convert to Judaism if this should be your wish. Oh no, Mr. Appleman," Andy shook his head in determination, "I have lived with this hope for too many years to just disappear out of your life. Esther needs me. We love each other. Can't you understand? Esther agreed to marry me and we won't take no for an answer, from you or anyone else. Please, Mr. Appleman, give us your blessing!" Andy pleaded.

"Not on your life!" Esther's father retorted. "It is said," he continued, in the tone of a prayer, "that a daughter most often brings misfortune and unhappiness to her parents, but I never for a moment believed that my daughter Esther would be one of those!" Raising his hands towards the ceiling, he lamented, "God of the Universe, I beg you to intervene on my behalf. Make them understand that they are on a path of self-destruction."

Everyone in the room remained silent for a few moments, then Andy began, carefully picking his words. "In a way I don't blame you. I understand. You are an orthodox, a prestigious respected member of a synagogue and the Jewish community. To you it would be considered a transgression against the Jewish law to even entertain the idea that your daughter is in love with an ordinary Ukrainian boy and is willing to marry him. You don't believe me, do you? Well, ask your daughter," he said, pointing with his finger.

Esther was curled up in a chair, holding a towel to her face to dry tears that were flowing uncontrollably, while her brother Bernie whispered words of encouragement to her. Sitting by a window staring into the night, Esther began to feel doubt for a brief moment. "What if my father is right?" she speculated. The life she would have to live if she were to surrender to his will flashed before her eyes. She saw her future by looking at her mother and the other women on the block. She would probably be compelled to marry some Chassidic boy, attend the ritual bath, bear children, grow old and stagnant, while the world outside remained so large, beautiful and inviting, full of expectation and excitement.

"If I married Andy," she thought, "I would live in a different world, with different, sophisticated people. I'm sure he would be good to me. We could travel, visit far-away places because he loves me. No," she shook her head, "I mustn't be intimidated by my father. It's my life and I want to live it my way!"

Mr. Appleman raised his hands towards the ceiling and began praying again. "God of our fathers, am I not a religious man? Am I not obeying your Ten Commandments? Am I not a devout Jew? Why are you punishing me? All my life I prayed three times daily, attended services in the house of worship. Why then am I destined to bear such sorrow and humiliation? Through the years I have dreamed a beautiful dream: visualizing my Esther marrying a nice orthodox boy, who on Fridays, the Sabbath or on Holy Days would be walking to the synagogue with me. It would have been the sweetest time of my life and that of my wife. It would have contributed great pride and joy to our lives!"

God didn't answer him. The attic remained painfully silent. No one dared to utter a word. Only the wind in the dark of night whistled under the loose shingle on the roof.

"Andy, she doesn't know what she is doing!" Mr. Appleman exploded again. "She is too young to know the true meaning of love. She is infatuated, confused by your constant flattery and attention. Remember my words! You will one day realize that what you're about to do is wrong. It'll haunt you for the rest of your life. You both deserve to be happily married into your own religion, your culture and customs of your people." He slowly turned to Esther and pleaded, "Are you listening, my child?"

"Yes", she whispered.

"Do you love Andy enough to give up your identity, forsake our way of life, and bring shame upon us?"

"I shall bring no shame on anyone by marrying the one I love!" Esther replied. "May he be Jewish, Irish or whatever. Love doesn't choose or reject religion or nationality. Andy is good and kind. Although Ukrainian, he might turn out to be a better Jew than you are, even though he doesn't wear a beard. You're my parents and I love you both dearly, but don't force me to live my life your way. The future is mine and I must do what I think is right for me even at the risk of losing you."

"How dare you speak to me this way!" her father shouted, incoherently. "Is this what I came to this country for? God, can you hear me? If you can, why don't you answer me?" He turned to Esther, his eyes blazing, looked at her and shouted "He isn't even circumcised!"

"I'll have it done, if that's what you want!" Andy interjected with noticeable embarrassment.

Bernie, who said nothing during the argument, turned to his father and asked calmly, "Why are you tormenting them? Why don't you leave them be? They have the right to live the kind of life they choose."

"You speak about rights regardless of how your mother and I feel about it. For the last time, Bernie, would you speak to your sister; maybe you can persuade her to change her mind!"

"I have already given you my opinion, I have nothing else to say," Bernie replied.

Mr. Appleman, totally exhausted, sat down on a kitchen chair and murmured,

"She said she was going to follow him. Where to? What more can I say? How can I punish her? Should I slap her face? No, anger will only make it worse."

Bernie cautiously approached his father and asked, "Can I tell you something?"

"Go ahead, I'm listening."

"Ever since Andy was a child he often expressed his love for Jewish people. He would watch Ma lighting the Sabbath candles on Friday evening, wishing his mother would do the same. You don't necessarily have to be Jewish to appreciate Judaism. Everyone regardless of religion appreciates some sanctity and a divine atmosphere in a home, that lights up for a few hours a dull daily existence. Pa, please," Bernie pleaded, "stop arguing. There is no other solution."

His father, however, ignored him and continued: "Don't you realize that she is about to throw her life away? And hurt the people closest to her who love her? And you are still insisting that I should agree to this crazy marriage so that we'll all be happy? Happiness is wonderful when it can be shared with family. Grief and sorrow are easier to bear when there are loved ones who can console each other. You refuse to understand what I am saying. Some day you will, but it'll be too late! Your mother and I sacrificed our lives to give you both a decent home, a good education. We taught you values, morals and principles, and now you're implying that I'm crazy?"

His face was deep red, and perspiration was glistening in the deep furrows of his forehead. His beard was ruffled like an overgrown bush after a storm and his eyes were ablaze. In desperation, he turned to his wife, Goldie, for moral support.

Mrs. Appleman was standing, huddled unobtrusively in a corner of the kitchen, her hands clasped tight in front of her as if in prayer.

"Nu, what do you think?" he demanded to know.

She took a deep breath, raised her head and replied, "I wish I could fully agree with you. But we must deal with the situation in a rational way. I think there comes a time when parents must realize that their children have grown up and have a right to make their own decisions, some of which will most likely be wrong, and will have an adverse effect on their future. Unfortunately, there is nothing we can do about it, except stand by and let them learn by their own mistakes."

"This is outrageous!" screamed her husband, hitting the table top with his fist. "My own wife has also turned against me. She has suddenly become a philosopher! No! No! I can't allow Esther to go through with this. I know it won't work!"

Suddenly, very calmly, he got down on his knees, embraced Esther and whispered softly "Please, my child, don't destroy your life!"

"But Papa, we love each other, nothing else matters!" she obstinately replied.

Mr. Appleman stood up, stepped back and in a voice matching the contempt coming out of his fiery eyes, replied, "I am now fully convinced that you are not about to change your mind. The only thing your mother and I can do is disown you. We will never reconcile ourselves to such a horrible nightmare. We would rather lose you than agree to your shameful act. We'll forget that we once had a daughter we loved, who is no longer a member of our people!" He slowly turned towards Esther and said in a low voice, "Forgive me for the things I have said here this evening, as it turned out it apparently was all in vain." He then turned to his wife:

"Goldie, I must go to the synagogue at once and say *Kaddish* after our Esther. To us she is dead! Andy, before I leave this room I must tell you that we never want to see you again, and you must

56

promise me that you'll not get married in this city. Go to a rabbi somewhere out of town and do not remain living here in Winnipeg!"

He opened the door and in a frenzy stormed out of the attic. His heavy footsteps echoed through the building and in a blinding rage he slammed the downstairs door behind him. Esther jumped to her feet and embraced Andy. Both were consciously aware of the electrifying moment for which they had been waiting for many years. Esther sighed and said "Andy, we must comply with my father's last wish. Let's prepare to leave town tomorrow."

The following morning they boarded a train and were together on their first journey of life, heading for Montreal. Esther put her head down on Andy's lap, looked up at him and asked, "How did your parents react when you told them about our marriage?"

"Well, my father took it philosophically. He said, 'My boy, you are old enough to handle your own life. It wouldn't be fair for me to interfere in spite of my negative feelings. I guess genuine love can't be concerned with religion or nationality, basically we are all the same.' My mother however, was stunned when I told her, but she too accepted it as a matter of my choice. "Hug me again," Andy whispered, "and together we'll live in a heaven of love."

They whispered promises while the train tried to catch the sun. It was a new beginning to an old dream. Yet, while she deeply loved Andy, she would never forget the parents who had disowned her and the brother who had supported her in the struggle for the right to live her own life. "May God help Bernie in his own search for happiness," she prayed.

CHAPTER 7

Bernie sat on the Salter bridge thinking. He was trying to recall the few joys, the sorrows and the frustrations he had endured for many years since the Applemans arrived in Winnipeg — all the episodes and events that touched his life and left indelible scars. Looking down at the expanse of the railroad tracks he vividly remembered the day his friend Finky bade him good-bye, jumped a freight train and headed west. Bernie wondered whether he had reached Vancouver as he had planned. Life hadn't been the same since but, in the last few years, time bridged the gap by bringing him even closer to his friend Andy.

Nostalgia triggered his emotions. "No one ever appreciates the present. Everything seems better when it's no more," he thought. He wondered how Andy and Esther were making out, wherever they were. They had not told him where they were intending to settle down. "My parents consider her dead," he thought. "Although it's very painful for me to think that I may never see her again, to me she is alive and always will be. No one ever dies as long as there is someone left to remember. When there is no one left, it really doesn't matter. I wish them luck, they certainly deserve it."

He began analyzing his own situation and his future. "I'm next in line to make my move. For me life is becoming more and more unbearable, especially since Esther left. I find it terribly depressing to be living where grief, sorrow and sadness are constantly present. It's eroding my mind. My parents are mourning the loss of Esther in a very special way which I can no longer bear. I am now the only survivor. All my friends have gone seeking new horizons. I don't really know how much longer I can endure this lonely existence. I too shall one day soon spread out my wings and fly away. My dreams, however, are more realistic than Finky's. I would be content to reach Edmonton or Calgary. But I must wait. The timing for such an adventure is very important."

As time passed, Bernie fought with his father daily. His father was intoxicated with Chassidic fanaticism and those radical beliefs were thrown mercilessly at Bernie.

"Where are you going now?" he would ask Bernie whenever the boy moved towards the front door.

"Out," Bernie would reply.

"It's too late for you to be on the streets."

"Father, ever since Esther married Andy, you've been on my back. Well, I'm not a child. I'm grown up and I can decide for myself when I go out and when I come back. Don't take out your anger over Esther on me. It was your choice to disown her, don't try to blame me for it!"

"Bernie," his father said, "Bernie, you're right." He embraced his son. "You're all the children I have left and I just can't bear to lose you as well." He stepped back, wiped a tear off his cheek and went to his room.

That night, Bernie decided it was time he left home. It didn't take him long to find a room near the Young Men's Hebrew Association where he had a job.

Late one evening, just before going to sleep, there was a knock on his door. It was a police officer.

"Are you Bernie Appleman?" the officer asked.

"Whatever it is I didn't do it!" he said with a smile.

"I'm Officer Patterson," he said with a stern face.

"Come in, officer. What can I do for you?"

"I have some bad news I'm afraid. Perhaps you'd better sit down." Bernie did as he was told.

"Your parents were involved in a car accident."

"O my God."

"It was on Main Street. They were struck by a car. I don't have any details except that they were rushed to St. Boniface Hospital."

"I must leave at once."

"I'm afraid they're in intensive care and no visitors are allowed."

"What am I to do? I just can't sit here and do nothing."

"Perhaps I could take you to your parents' home. You could pack some of their things to make their stay at the hospital a little more comfortable."

"Yes, yes, I would like to do that." Bernie said still stunned by the news. He dressed quickly while the officer waited patiently.

"I just thought of something. Could we pick up Yurko Posarek on the way? He's my sisters' father-in-law and the only family I have to turn to right now."

"Yes. No problem."

They picked up Yurko and filled him in then drove to the attic apartment which belonged to Bernie's parents. It was two in the morning when the officer left them.

"I'll return as soon as there's news. Goodnight." he said and tapped a salute with one finger.

The night felt like an eternity to Bernie and Yurko and when the officer returned the following morning, the expression on his face told them what he was about to say.

"I'm sorry, Bernie."

"It's over?"

"This morning at 7:04."

Bernie's knees buckled and Yurko rushed in to hold him up. He helped Bernie to the bed in the adjoining room where he watched as the young man dissolved in tears.

The following day, in early afternoon, he was driven to the cemetery where most of the members of the Rumanian synagogue were present. Some were sobbing quietly, others were crying openly. Bernie, however, was unable to talk or cry. He stood, detached, wondering why he had been brought there. He stayed like that for days while friends came and went from the attic. When they stopped coming he began to absorb what had actually happened and the full impact of the tragedy descended upon him. Loneliness, grief and despair finally penetrated his emotions while his life was becoming more solitary every day. Instead of going to work, he would stay in his attic. His heart was numb and the blood in his veins had turned to ice. Yurko came to be with him often.

"How devastatingly ironic life can be," Bernie said one evening, "Finky's father also passed away when it was bitter cold. His mother too is gone, died of a broken heart. My parents, who swore by everything that's holy never to see Esther again or mention her name, are also gone. They are no longer subjected to the pain, the suffering, the sorrow of losing a daughter. Now their oath will never be broken. I'm the only one left. I must leave this God-forsaken city just as soon as spring arrives".

"Where to?" Yurko asked

"Anywhere," Bernie replied.

The weeks and months dragged by as if winter would never end. But the day finally came when the birds returned, singing, dancing, twittering along the boughs of sun-spattered trees in Kildonan Park. As life around him was renewed, Bernie again felt confidence in himself and was prepared to meet destiny head-on.

CHAPTER 8

The years were kind to Finky. He thrived on the luxuries which Helga provided. He was also quite successful in business ventures. A new life, a new world, had opened up for him since the day he met Helga. They travelled around the world many times and were guests of nobility in some countries. One day she informed him that she would like to tour Madrid, and, for some excitement, see a bull fight.

"Every time she speaks it's like music to my ears", he smiled with satisfaction. "She looks beautiful and refreshing like a rose in a gentle rain. There is grace in her step, heaven in her blue eyes and she projects dignity with every gesture." Suddenly, a trace of guilt crossed his mind. "Do I really love her, or am I using her for my own gains? Is it gratitude that I am feeling, disguised as love? I'm sure though that in time I'll truly and genuinely love her. She is beautiful."

He turned to her: "Helga, you are the most unusual woman I've met and I love you."

She caressed his lower lip, his chin. "I'll make you a millionaire if you let me. I promise," she whispered.

"I'll let you, I swear," Finky jokingly replied. "Will it really happen, I mean, will I really be wealthy one day?"

"Trust me," she replied. "You are young, good looking, ambitious and most of all, you're my prince. I'll do everything I can to help you achieve your goal in life. You have great potential which I intend to cultivate and make you rich in the process!" She embraced him again and together they were lost in a swirling hypnotic spell of passion.

That evening, she told him about her villa on the beach of Malaga, where the trees were green and tranquil, and the whispering surf licked the sun-drenched beaches, bringing total serenity to one's heart. But one thing from Finky's past continued to bother her and Helga chose this moment to resolve it.

"From today on, your name shall not be 'Finky'. It's a nickname for a kid, not for a mature man who is on the threshold of becoming a tycoon in the business world. As of today, your name will be Ruben Finkel. It has a prestigious ring to it."

"Thank you Helga, you're my Messiah."

"Don't thank me just yet, this is only the beginning," she replied teasingly, pinching his cheek.

Among European capitals, Madrid is certainly comparable to Rome or Paris. It retains a certain crispness and sparkle, particularly on bright spring or autumn days, when the wind clears the air of smog. Spaniards enjoy life. The villas in the old town attract a bohemian subculture—students, authors, bawds with their whores, and back door smugglers all do a roaring business.

While they enjoyed the sights and pleasures of the great city, Helga made sure they saw a bull fight as planned. She found it exciting and entertaining watching toreadors and agitated bulls perform. To put Ruben more at ease, she tactfully chatted about the spectacle during the ride to the arena. "Bull fights are usually staged during religious feasts or festivals," she explained. "They take place in different parts of the country at different times of the season. Capes, which are part of the uniform, are called 'muletas' which prominent matadors wear with their colourful regalia during a performance. It is a dangerous art, fighting a bull, while thousands are cheering for the kill."

It was a very hot Sunday. The stands were packed to capacity. Picadors on horses rode around in the arena, inciting the bulls to the brink of madness. Trumpets suddenly erupted in a deafening blast. The excitement mounted. The restless mass of humanity whistled and shouted, "Matador, matador." Hysteria rose with each passing minute. A matador appeared, dressed in a glittering costume of blood-red satin, trimmed with royal blue and gold. Disdainfully, he flung open his red cape as he bowed to the thousands of half-mad spectators who had come to witness the most gory act of inhumanity and bestiality. In Hispanic tradition, he began waving the cape in front of the enraged animal while the Spaniards screamed. Every time the bull charged towards him he gracefully stepped out of the way until, finally, he speared the tired animal to death.

For Ruben and Helga, it was an exciting afternoon. Afterwards, they drove back to the villa which was situated on a private beach along the Mediterranean shore. Other villas shared the strand but, to Ruben, Helga's was the nicest of all. They returned to prepare for yet another dinner party. Ruben assumed this was how the wealthy lived — entertainment during the day, parties every other night. But he also had a feeling that he was being groomed to take his place beside Helga among the international social elite.

With every passing day, his confidence increased. He had closed a few real estate deals, acting as Helga's agent and partner, which made him feel proud and important. His impossible dream had become an incredible reality. "And this is only the beginning," he remembered her saying.

One afternoon, the sun was shining brightly, and they were enjoying the comfort of their patio and the turquoise clear water in the swimming pool. Ruben rested his head on his sweetheart's lap and asked, "Helga, do you really love me?"

"What a silly question!" she reproached him gently. "Haven't I proved my love to you in so many ways?"

"Of course you have," he replied. "I need to know for sure though. I am afraid that this is a dream, and when I wake up one day it'll be gone."

"Don't worry, my darling, this dream will continue for as long as we both shall live. Trust me. I have more surprises for you that will materialize in due course." She looked at him with love in her eyes and asked, "Are you prepared to be mine until the end of time?"

"Dear Helga, you are beautiful, charming and wealthy. Give me one good reason why I shouldn't? How about you?" he asked her in return.

"Let's just say that I am prepared to love you forever. I think that I have proved it thus far."

"Of course you have. How foolish of me to doubt your sincerity," Ruben apologized.

She pressed him tightly to her bosom, kissed him passionately and said, "Let's freshen up in the swimming pool."

"Why not?" Ruben agreed half-jokingly.

Without another word he picked her up, cradling her in his arms like a child and carried her into the pool. He felt her cool soft hands caressing his body while a strange burning sensation made his heart beat like a hammer.

The following day Pierre drove them to Madrid. Helga took Ruben into her lawyer's office where a document had been prepared for her signature. She signed it, held it in her hand, turned to Ruben and said, "I have a surprise for you." Not waiting for his response she handed him the document.

"What is this?" he asked.

"This, my dear, is a deed to a half-interest in everything I own, which, I might add, is quite substantial. It's yours from this day on!"

"This is indeed a passport to the world," he thought. "I only wish my friends and those who called me 'bum' in Winnipeg could see me now! However, this is hardly the time to dwell on past, dried-up memories. They're totally insignificant at this point in my life. There is a proverb I have heard many times: 'Whatever your mind believes, you can achieve.' I have always been a great believer of having faith in yourself but now I'm totally convinced that this saying is without a doubt true in every way. I can now look back at those gray and hopeless years of my life and laugh out loud if I want to."

Suddenly, he was aware that others were looking at him. Ruben took Helga in his arms and kissed her tenderly. "My dear," he said, "today you have made me the happiest man in the world. The only way I can express my gratitude is to promise you, again, my unending love and devotion."

"How sweet of you. Thank you, Ruben. I'll remember your words and hope that you will too," she remarked calmly.

Ruben hoped that, after being made a partner in Helga's estate, they would end the many years of travelling and choose a place to settle down and take it easy for a while. Helga, however, loved to travel. Ruben was well aware that her restless soul urged her on to explore new worlds, new customs and captivating horizons. He was, therefore, both surprised and grateful when Helga, too, was beginning to show signs of exhaustion.

"My dear Ruben," she said one day, "would you mind if we were to go to Stockholm and settle down for a change? We could live a domestic life and let time slowly go by."

"It's O.K. with me," he agreed. "In fact, I have been thinking about it myself."

For the journey to Sweden, Ruben handled all the travel arrangements for the first time. Ruben was secretly pleased, especially when he noticed that his orders were carried out with the same quiet efficiency that Helga had always received. The real estate deals, the partnership, and now the servants — it was gradually all coming his way, with Helga as his lover and his guardian angel!

Ruben and Helga travelled to what they hoped might be their final home in their favourite way — first class passage in a cruise ship. They paid little heed to the news reports of Nazi German belligerence and the fear of war that was spreading across Europe and the British Isles. For Helga and Ruben it was a perfect summer as they boarded the ship for a leisurely voyage to Stockholm. They spent the first evening at sea on deck under shimmering stars. They danced to the lilting rhythm of Viennese waltzes played by the ship's orchestra. It was a fairy tale reverie which was shattered by a strident voice on the loud speakers.

"Attention, please — attention everyone! This is the captain with an important message. I have just received some bad news. The German army has invaded Poland. At this very moment Warsaw and Krakow are being bombed. I will advise you of important developments as I receive them."

On deck, passengers huddled in small groups and voiced their fear and helplessness in the wake of this news. Then the captain was heard again.

"In view of the circumstances we are proceeding to Nice. You may disembark there and go on to Switzerland by train if you wish."

Within a few days Ruben and Helga, with Pierre, found themselves in the Swiss city of Berne, where they decided to stay until they could sort out the news and see how it might affect them. Perhaps they might be spared the horrors of war if they remained in Switzerland.

From the beginning of their stay in Berne, news reports of the war were gloomy and became worse every day. The Nazis unleashed devastating bombing attacks on Poland and, as the war spread, upon other small or ill-prepared countries which they conquered with little resistance. Jews, along with any others opposed to Hilter's bestial philosophy, were slaughtered in their homelands or were shipped like cattle to concentration camps to be destroyed. It was a concerted attempt at total annihilation of innocent people so that, according to Hitler's plan set out in *Mein Kampf*, a pure Aryan race would populate and control the world.

In the shelter of the Alps, safe, but surrounded by warring armies, Helga and Ruben listened to radio broadcasts and read the newspapers with increasing horror as the civilized world seemed to be tearing itself apart. Fortunately for them, their business and financial assets were safe in neutral Spain and Sweden. They were able to draw upon them and enjoy reasonable comfort in Berne. Although doubtless they could have made their way to Madrid or Stockholm, they decided they should not take the risk and would wait out the hostilities that were wrecking Europe.

It was six years before Helga and Ruben contemplated the wisdom of moving to Stockholm. The war obviously was near its end. Hitler was dead, his insane empire was crushed, his armies beaten. The Japanese had surrendered after the destruction of Hiroshima by the atomic bomb. When at last it was safe to travel again, Helga's agent in Sweden was instructed to put her villa in order and she, Ruben and Pierre made their way there just as soon as a ship became available.

Helga's Swedish home was outside Stockholm, on Lake Malaren near the Baltic Sea. On sunny days, she and Ruben would spend a couple of hours on the beach, then retreat to the air-conditioned house. But it became increasingly obvious that Helga was not well. Her face little by little became thinner, her provocative smile was dimming, her once sparkling eyes were dull. Summers came and went. Indeed, all the seasons left their distinct marks especially on Helga. Ruben's black and curly hair was now mixed with gray, a few lines were beginning to show on his face, he was not as sprightly as he had been. But he had matured with dignity and that showed in his face and his bearing.

They lived a relatively quiet life now and only on rare occasions did they invite a few close friends to dinner.

Despite the ailments of time, Helga was still a beautiful woman, her figure trim, her style elegant. It never showed that she was ten years older than Ruben. Unhappily, beauty could not stop the invasion of ill-health. Helga complained of constant headaches. She would not go swimming or even relax at the side of the pool. Gradually she lost interest in the beach and then, in life.

It was apparent to Ruben that Helga did not want to worry him and was forcing her smile in his presence. Ruben insisted she see a doctor. After the examination, the doctor confided in Ruben:

"Sir, I am by no means a pessimist", he said cautiously. "But I do feel that it is my duty to inform you that Helga is a very sick woman. There is an embolism dangerously close to her brain and very little can be done for her. Although I promised her not to tell you, I think you ought to know."

During her illness, Helga and Ruben talked about many things, including her finances. She always tried to avoid speaking about the obvious, trying (although not really succeeding) to impress upon Ruben that there was nothing wrong with her that a long rest wouldn't cure. As though to prove that she was right,

Helga began to take long walks every day around the gardens with Ruben. The walks became a regular part of their day. When, as he did from time to time, Ruben suggested they take their strolls in other places, Helga, smiling sadly, gently insisted that they remain in her own gardens. "It reminds me of Stanley Park, where we met", she once said. Every time Ruben would try to change the route or place he would be gently rebuffed, he would smile back, take her arm in his and together they would stroll the paths for yet another time. When the weather was good, they would end their walk by having tea in the summer house near the villa's lakeside entrance. Helga would rest a few minutes by herself while Ruben returned to the villa to fetch the tea cart the servants had prepared.

Daily exercise seemed to bring the bloom back to her complexion and her eyes seemed brighter but Ruben was uncertain. Was it a change in health or was it Helga's desperation to hang on to life? Each day, when he went for the tea cart, he would try to decide which it was. Finally, he got an answer.

One day, as he was about to leave her, Helga held on to his arm a trifle longer than usual. A look he did not understand flashed across her eyes, then faded as quickly as it came. Something told him to stay but Helga urged him to get the tea as was his custom. She was only a little tired, she said. He returned to a limp and lifeless body that was once his Helga. In his brief absence, she had quietly, gently, slipped into eternity.

Ruben broke down. Although he didn't shed a tear, he felt that with Helga's passing, his world fell apart. He was bitter, angry, sad and frightened. Not once in all the years did he ever anticipate such a tragic ending.

On Helga's tombstone Ruben ordered the following epitaph:
"My Dear Helga.
If love could have saved,
you would have lived."

For several months, Ruben was immersed in grief, anguish and self-pity. Gradually, things became clearer in his mind and he thought: "Everyone is ultimately alone. Although I have many friends I am not about to start searching for sympathetic faces to console me. She left me a lifetime of wonderful memories." It occurred to him that Helga had given him love, happiness and devotion. She made life enjoyable. Each day was wrapped in a beautiful rainbow and the sun shone, even on rainy days.

"Life without her will be unbearable," he thought. "I'm alone. Empty ..." Ruben was suddenly afraid. "Pierre!" he shouted, "Pierre, where are you?"

Pierre rushed into the room.

"What good am I without her?" Ruben screamed.

"Calm yourself down, sir," Pierre pleaded. "What's gone can't be recaptured. I'm here. There is a cook and a maid. You'll make out. Give yourself some time to get adjusted to a different kind of life."

"You know, Pierre, I had never really tasted pride or success until I met Helga. I only wish I could tell her just one more time. Why did she leave me, tell me? Couldn't we have planned to go together?"

Suddenly as if in a terrifying panic, he threw on some clothes and said, "Pierre, please walk me to the beach."

Thoughts kept tumbling in his head in disarray. Nothing mattered any longer: his appearance, his financial position, not even his health.

He recalled the hot summer days, the pleasure of walking with Helga on the soft warm sand, watching the waves, foamy and wrinkled, gently rolling towards the beach, licking and caressing the glistening sand, gazing at white sailboats out at sea, and listening to the cry of seagulls. It all seemed like an endless holiday in paradise, where dreams and reality were united.

Some time later, he found himself walking barefoot back and forth on the beach. The sand was cool. Everything was still enveloped in silent semi-darkness, broken only by the whispering sounds of water ripples licking the sand. The deserted beach extended like a strip of paradise into the hazy distance. He looked up to the fading moon and stars: "I wonder in what form Helga's soul may soon be drifting in the mysterious universe?" he said aloud.

A passage he once read came to mind:

"I am ablaze with a thousand centuries of
suns. I am at this time compressed into
one small capsule of stillness while ravaging
forces are in the process of destroying me.
I'll not perish. I am older than star-light
and must make peace with time."

"Even though I'm aware it'll be difficult, perhaps even impossible," Ruben reflected, "I'm promising Helga now that I'll never stop trying."

Early one morning, Ruben, his mind steeped in sorrow, paced up and down the beach at Malaren. In the east, the sun, covered by a fine transparent haze, was slowly rising, reflecting pink splashes on the yearning horizon. He was totally unaware of what was going on around him — unaware until a voice woke him from his reverie.

"Good morning, you don't sleep nights, do you?" the voice said.

Ruben lost in grief was startled, he turned around and looked at the stranger. It was a young man, tall, handsome, longish hair neatly combed, ruggedly athletic in body. The stranger spoke again, in what Ruben knew was Swedish.

"Sorry, I don't speak Swedish", Ruben said.

The man spoke again, this time in English tinged with the accent of the Nordic tongue.

"I don't think we've met before", Ruben responded. "You're Swedish, I suppose."

"Yes, I was born and raised near here."

"Your English is good, the little I've heard. How come?"

"Oh, I've been around. Some time I can tell you more if we can get better acquainted. I've seen you here so often that I feel I know you personally. Perhaps we could get to know each other, even be friends."

At that, Ruben thought, "If I ever needed a friend, it's now". Aloud, he said, "You're so tanned you must be here a lot. What brings you here? Don't you have a job?"

"Yes, I have one, but it's not the sort you're probably thinking a fellow like me would have. I'll be entirely frank with you: I am a male prostitute and I'm also what you call in English, I think, a pimp."

Ruben was surprised that the young man should so readily describe his activities, which were usually not discussed in polite society and not with such candour with a stranger. "What got you into that?" he asked.

"My father died when I was very young. My mother had to go out to work if we were to survive. In fact, she still works, as a waitress. I quit school when I was fourteen. I hung around with boys much older than I was. Some of them were ..." The stranger hesitated, unable to find the word in his English vocabulary. "Do you mean 'queer' perhaps?" Ruben suggested. "Yes, that's it, they were 'queer'," said the young man.

Ruben and he chatted together on a variety of topics, during which conversation Ruben learned that he was talking to Ingmar Johansen, known as Ingi to his friends. Ingi was told that his new acquaintance was Ruben Finkel, and very little more at that time. Half an hour later they went their separate ways, after each expressed the hope that they would meet again.

They did meet again, the next day, and on several ensuing afternoons. As they talked, they grew to like and accept each other and it seemed that what had been a most casual meeting might develop into a lasting friendship, despite the irregularity of the life that Ingi led and the austere career in business that Ruben had embarked upon.

"Do you really mean that women pay you for sleeping with them?" Ruben asked Ingi one day in genuine curiosity.

"No, not really", Ingi replied with a laugh. "I'm a member of a club that supplies me with information as to who wants what. I serve many with mixed sexual desires. I procure hookers of both sexes for those who want variety in their sexual relationships."

"Who are your customers?" Ruben inquired, his interest fully aroused.

"All kinds of people, men and women who are looking for

excitement in various forms. They may be truck drivers or they may be judges. During the tourist season I do a big business when people have an opportunity to cheat a little. They're all looking for the same thing: temporary romance and sexual gratification to brighten up their boring lives."

"Do you indulge in any offbeat sex yourself?" Ruben asked, this time with some hesitation. Ingi, however, was not bothered by the query.

"When you are serving liquor, you're bound to taste it once in a while, even though you may not be a steady drinker."

Ingi decided it was time for him to ask a question or two.

"Your name is Ruben Finkel. That's so formal. Haven't you ever had a nickname?" he asked.

"Yes, for years I was called Finky, but I promised Helga that I would insist on being called Ruben. And that's the way I want it."

"Okay, it's Ruben with me", said Ingi. "Now may I ask who is Helga?"

"Not is — was", said Ruben, his face clouding over in recollecting his recent loss.

"Sorry", Ingi hastened to say. "I'm sorry I touched on a sensitive subject."

Ruben assured Ingi that he was not upset by the question, he was upset by the most innocent mention of the name of one he had loved so dearly and had so tragically lost. Ruben told Ingi of the long and happy relationship he had had with a woman he deeply loved. "She gave me everything I ever wanted", he said.

Toward the end of the day, Ingi invited Ruben to go with him to a party at the home of one of the club members.

"It won't be the kind of party you usually attend," Ingi gave warning.

"The world is full of experiments," Ruben replied accepting the invitation.

From the moment he entered the huge party room, Ruben felt uncomfortable and even apprehensive. Drinks of every description were served continuously, an orchestra played without respite, there was a floor show featuring men in "drag" and almost nude women. It became too much for Ruben to bear. "What would Helga say?" he thought. He pleaded a severe headache and left for home.

The next day he apologized to Ingi for his sudden departure. "There was just too much perversion for someone like me", he explained.

Despite the differences in their lives and temperaments, the two gradually became close friends. They saw each other almost every day and enjoyed each other's conversation and company. Then, one day, for the first time Ruben invited Ingi to dinner at the mansion he had inherited. "I've never seen a place like this before", said Ingi in wonderment as he entered the ornate entrance hall.

After they had dined, Ruben said: "Ingi, as you know, since Helga's death I have led a very lonely life. Meeting you and developing a friendship with you has meant a lot to me, more than you could ever realize. Now I'm wondering if it could be put on a more solid basis. If I were to ask you to live here with me, what would you say?" Then he hastened to add, before Ingi could answer, "This has absolutely nothing to do with sex!"

Ingi took a moment or two to think before replying,

"I don't really know if I could ever get used to living in such luxury," he said, looking about the elegant dining room. "This is heaven in comparison to the place I live in. I'm not sure I could change my ways."

"Will you please think about it!" Ruben urged his guest.

"I don't have to think about it, I'm going to accept your kind and generous offer. If I don't agree right now, I might wake up and find that this was only a dream."

The next day Ingi moved his modest belongings into Ruben's villa and became an accepted member of the household. Ruben was so interested in Ingi's mode of life away from his new home that when Ingi got back each night, no matter how late, he was invited to tell Ruben in detail about the people he had met and the experiences he had had. After one such narration of his news, Ingi summoned up his courage and asked Ruben if he could have one or two of his friends over at the house. To this request Ruben immediately agreed and replied "Anyone who is your friend is welcome to this house."

That weekend, Ingi escorted an attractive woman to dinner. She was slender, with a striking figure, a smooth face and blond hair intermixed with silver gray. Her name was Susan. She contributed much to the dinner table conversation and Ruben found her so interesting that he invited her to come again. This she did, more than once. Ruben welcomed her with open arms and, as he began to look forward to her presence with increasing pleasure, he thought, "This girl makes me forget my sorrow by just being here. She really is helping me lessen the sadness that still gnaws at my heart."

Then one evening, Ingi received an urgent telephone call and asked if he could borrow Ruben's car to attend to an urgent matter. "I'll be back in two or three hours", he said, as he drove off.

Susan was over that evening and Ruben asked her to join him in the living room. Pierre brought in a bottle of wine and glasses, then tip-toed out of sight. After a few glasses of wine, Ruben felt unusually warm and when he complained of the heat, Susan said she would make him comfortable. She soaked a towel in cold water and applied it to his forehead.

An almost forgotten feeling began to arise in Ruben and he could not resist the desire to embrace his guest. They locked together in a long, passionate kiss. Then Ruben took Susan's hand and whispered, the words incoherent, "Come with me, my dear — come with me to the bedroom. It's much cooler there ..."

When Ingi returned, he found them both sitting on the balcony and one look at them satisfied him that the scheme he had devised to bring Ruben and Susan together had worked.

"Should I drive you home now, or would you rather stay here?" he asked with a sly smile. "Please take me home, if you will," Susan replied.

Ruben was sure now that Ingi had planned the whole affair, and he was grateful for it. Susan visited the house again and again.

But the best of things almost always eventually come to an end, and the relationship with Susan had to be terminated for one very special reason. Ruben, after much thought, decided he would return to his grass roots and go back to Canada.

What to do about Ingi and Pierre? Ruben asked Ingi to accompany him. Ingi was delighted with the idea and accepted at once. Ruben offered the same opportunity to Pierre.

"I've been with and served Miss Helga and you all my working life", Pierre said, "But I'm getting on in years and changing countries at my age wouldn't be practical. I'll remain here where I really belong. But thank you for asking me, and having me with you. I have enjoyed my life and I'll be forever grateful to you and Miss Helga for making it all possible."

The two clasped their arms around each other like brothers and, as Pierre stepped back, he brushed a tear from Ruben's lapel.

CHAPTER 9

Ruben's destination was Winnipeg, but Ingi insisted that Montreal was the place for him. Ruben reluctantly bowed to his friend's wishes and, through connections, found a sales position for Ingi with a car dealer.

As he was alone in a place with so many different memories, Ruben was reminded of the oath he had taken when he jumped the freight train. A promise never to return to Winnipeg. Yet now, for some irrational reason, he was both saddened and elated to be back in the city he had left so many decades before.

The city had not really changed much during his absence. The streets appeared to be the same, only the faces of people were strange. He felt he had been away for a thousand years.

One of the first things he did was to buy a luxurious limousine, complete with a bar. He also wanted a chauffeur just like Pierre. It took days to find the suitable man. When at last he made his choice, he asked the new employee for his first name.

"Peter", the man replied.

"If you don't mind, and I don't know why you should, I would like to call you Pierre", said Ruben. The chauffeur agreed.

The recollection of the first Pierre revived memories of Helga. Ruben remembered how he had abandoned the nickname Finky at her request. How he wished Helga was with him now.

Although ill and emotionally drained, Ruben went to his office and sat at his desk. He made an attempt to look at his mail, then tossed it aside. His vision was blurred and the words appeared to play tricks on the page — they ran into each other or jumped over one another. There was a gentle rap on the door.

"Come in, it's open", he said.

"Shall I take you home, sir?" Pierre asked.

Ruben took Pierre's arm and walked slowly to the limousine.

"Pierre, you are an intelligent chap," Ruben said. "Tell me, have you ever thought about freedom and what it really means? Or how important it is to be free?"

"Well ..., no, sir, I never really have."

"I always thought that to be free would be some sort of achievement. I never realized though how painful and lonely freedom could be. How important am I really in the grand scheme of life? Tell me, Pierre," Ruben insisted.

"Sir, if I may express my opinion, I would say that it's wonderful how nature creates harmony within ourselves in time of sorrow and grief. It numbs our senses until such time when our consciousness is capable of absorbing the impact of a tragedy."

"Perhaps you are right," Ruben replied. "I never really thought about it that way! Pierre, please drop me off on Main Street. Perhaps a brisk walk will do me some good and I badly need some fresh air."

"Yes, sir", his chauffeur obediently replied.

He drove off and Ruben slowly walked along Main Street. It was a clear warm night. The deep blue sky was high and the traffic was heavy in spite of the late hour. A blinking red light above a saloon door on a side street drew his attention. In his depressed state he decided to observe it at closer range, curious to see what it was like inside.

At the entrance area, prostitutes lingered, watching the johns like skilled hunters stalking deer. They selectively appraised the drifters, lumberjacks, winos and the ever present thrill seekers. Ruben entered the saloon, sat down at the bar and out of the stench and smoke a husky bartender appeared.

"What'll you have?" he growled in a hoarse voice.

Ruben looked up to face an ugly giant of a man towering over him. His mouth was large, his lips were thick and a smouldering cigar was sticking out from between his yellow teeth.

"You sound like a real bastard. I barely sat down. Give me a few minutes to catch my breath!" Ruben protested.

"This is a joint where guys come in to drink. If you want to catch your breath, go to Kildonan Park and fly a kite!" he snarled.

"Give me some poison on the rocks," Ruben said in disgust.

"You think you're a wise guy or somethin?" the bartender asked in a menacing voice, "or are you some smart ass — too good for this joint? I've never seen you here before and I have a feeling you don't belong here. You either say what you want, or I'll toss you out on your ass!"

"O.K., give me a double rye." He gulped it down, ordered another one, and moved over to a table.

A blond hooker slithered over, sat down beside him and said, "Hello sport, aren't you going to buy a lady a drink?"

Ruben looked around and asked, "Where is the lady?"

"Me, silly."

"Do I owe you one?"

"Not really, but you would be well rewarded if you did."

Looking around the hazy, smelly saloon, he was suddenly obsessed with a frightening intuition that something was about to happen to him, while the hooker was reaching for his hand, trying to entice him to follow her.

"Come on, big boy, don't be shy," she hissed like a snake.

He was very much tempted to follow her but sheepishly resisted, telling her to get lost. Although he was too light-headed to think rationally, he suddenly remembered Helga. "If she were to see me now, I would bury myself with shame," he thought.

He remained sitting in deep contemplation. An image from the past formed in front of his blood-shot eyes. He studied it for a while. His father's face, that he hadn't seen in over fifty years, hazily began forming in front of him. He squinted, wiped his eyes to clear his vision, but the image was there, clearer than before. "Impossible!" he thought. He wanted to reach out, but restrained himself, hypnotized by the incredible ghost-like image. It was terribly wrinkled as he remembered his father too and partially covered by a skimpy yellow beard. Watery but penetrating eyes stared at him. He closed his eyes hoping the image would disappear. When he looked up again he could see it slowly dissolving into the saloon smoke. He heaved a sigh of relief, rested his head on both hands supported by the table, and murmured, "This is unbelieveable. He appeared at the precise time when I was considering the possibility of going with blondy to her room. If I were a religious man, I would attribute this phenomenon to spiritual forces which could inject into human consiousness a certain form of moral awareness in time's of utter despair." Ruben stared into space and was surprised by a female throaty voice.

"Hey," she shouted, "why are you so pale? Have you seen a ghost or somethin?" She cuddled up to him and asked, "Tell me, why are you such an old idiot? You could have a good time you know, if you wanted to."

"That's just it, I don't want to."

"The least you could do is offer me a drink," she innocently remarked.

"Yeah, I'll do that. Hey, waiter!" he shouted, "water on the rocks, mixed with arsenic," while going into convulsions of laughter.

She retreated, saying, "I hope you get termites in your pants, stupid old bugger!"

Ruben leaned over, took her hand, pulled her closer and whispered, "I'll tell you a secret! Promise you'll tell no one. Termites is all I got left in my pants!" He burst out into laughter again. She slapped his face and disappeared behind a swinging door. He put his hands tightly to his ears trying to blot out the sickening shrieking music forcing its way out of a juke box.

"Come on, pops, I'm ready when you are."

Ruben dizzily turned around and saw an olive-faced woman leaning over him from behind. She was ugly, and yet inviting, her eyes sparkling as if they were on fire. She wore a red band around her head and a floor length, oriental style, red dress. The bodice of the dress had been cut out revealing generous but sagging breasts.

"Go to the devil," he whispered thickly through clenched

teeth, and realized that he had a mouthful of tongue and that he was drunk.

"Don't be silly — take my advice. Soak it in sour milk and you will be as good as new!"

"You're joshing me," Ruben mumbled.

"I'm not joshing. Try it. You got nothing to lose."

He smiled crookedly, "Your kind makes my faucet shrink! This joint appears to be crawling with whores," he murmured. "Come to think of it, I have never been inside a whore house. I always went first-class. But now, my hair, what's left of it, is gray. My face is dried up like a raisin. Any slut would do, I guess. Perhaps I could still find some gratification in the arms of a hooker. On the other hand, to me sex is like a merry-go-round: it takes a long time to get on and it's over before you know it, you then wonder why you had the desire to get on in the first place." Although he believed that perhaps a sexual act would restore his self-confidence, he couldn't dare be unfaithful to his Helga again even though she was no longer here.

He slowly, awkwardly, slid out from behind the table, stumbled out into the street and made his way to the corner where he was to wait for Pierre to pick him up. Leaning against a wall, watching traffic slowly go by and a few lights agonizingly shining on the dismal streets, he stood, in an alcoholic daze, until Pierre arrived.

Back in his penthouse suite, he sat down heavily and began thinking.

"Why am I torturing myself with the irretrievable past and ghost-like images? I should rather turn my thoughts to more positive thinking if I am to survive. I should be proud of the success I have enjoyed in business ventures during my active years. For about forty years I have lived a life that seemed impregnable, although it suddenly collapsed and gave way to grief, sorrow and despair — but nothing lasts forever."

He thought of a book he once read during the years he was basking in glory and love with his beautiful Helga. He remembered a quotation in the prologue of Bertrand Russell's

What Have I Lived For:

"These passions, simple but overwhelmingly
strong, have governed my life; the longing
for love and the search for success. Those
passions, like great winds, have blown me in
a wayward course over deep oceans of anguish
reaching to the very verge of despair."

After a restless, broken sleep, Ruben awoke exhausted. He looked about the bedroom. Although the air-conditioned apartment was lavishly furnished, he found it indescribably depressing, even though the verdant grass below was silently singing and a myriad of flowers in their beds were smiling in the summer haze.

Memories he thought long dormant clawed at his brain, making a frustrated old man out of him. The thought of going to his office for a few hours made him feel ill. He looked out the window and imagined the world was spinning. His knees shook and his head throbbed. "It's no use," he thought, and felt that he could not go out in his present condition.

He began to realize with increasing clarity that his life had, in a way, been wasted in an unending struggle for wealth and respectability. He was, of course, proud of his achievements, but doubted at the same time whether it was worth the price he had paid. "It's too late for remorse," he thought, even though he felt he would gladly surrender his fortune if he could only recapture some of the years he had wasted on accumulating wealth.

He closed his eyes and childhood memories came into focus again. The horses, the cows, the shabby barns, and the awesome endless prairies in bright sunshine. He could visualize the wheat turning golden in late summer. He leaned back, trying to block out past years, but memories kept surfacing, gnawing at his heart. He covered his face with his hands and fell asleep.

He dreamed that he was flying through black space faster and faster, deeper and deeper into a bottomless pit, while, at the same time, he was thinking about Andy, Bernie and Esther. Esther was as beautiful as a budding rose. Ruben wondered whether Andy had succeeded in marrying her.

A tap on his shoulder brought him back to reality. He was staring at a familiar face, but couldn't remember the name at first. "Excuse me, sir. It is four o'clock in the afternoon. You have slept for many hours. I thought you might want to be awakened."

Ruben studied the face for a few dazed seconds, then exclaimed, "Oh, it's you Pierre! Thank you. I appreciate your concern." He took hold of Pierre's arm and both walked out on to the balcony. Pierre excused himself and left.

For an immeasurable length of time Ruben remained on the balcony, deep in thought and speculation:

"There's really no relationship between life and death — they are of separate planes. There is no point of contact between existence and non-existence; it's an endless chain, made up of billions of links since the beginning of time."

Neither a scholarly nor an intellectual person, who had never thought of the natural order of things or of the universe in general, Ruben now found himself more and more often pondering the imponderable. That evening, however, he was fascinated by the moon and stars above him. He felt that he had become a part of the inexplicable cosmos, where, perhaps, worlds were created and destroyed each minute of each day. He studied the face of the full moon, mesmerized by what he saw. He tried to figure out the Milky Way, but gave up after a few minutes.

"What's the use?" he asked himself. "I can't possibly comprehend any of this. I might as well focus my attention on things that are easier to understand."

A strip of white fluffy cloud drifted across the moon and vanished while a summer breeze caressed his face. "Perhaps," he thought, "a wind like this centuries ago brushed over King David's harp while it hung in his tent."

It was a clear night, the streets were almost deserted. Ruben looked down and the blinking traffic lights caught his attention. They were playing a game with each other — from green to amber, to red, to green and to amber again, winking, blinking in the dark of night. He was fascinated by it all, as if he had never seen it before.

Pierre appeared from the apartment and asked, "Would you perhaps like to go for a short spin in the car? I'm sure you would feel better."

"It's a good idea," Ruben replied.

Pierre helped him into his limousine. Ruben pressed a button and the bar door slid open. He took a drink of cognac, leaned back and tried to relax. His trembling hands, however, made him realize that his condition was deteriorating. "I feel as though I'm about to have a heart attack," he murmured. After a few minutes he called Pierre. "Would you please drive me back home?"

"Yes sir," his chauffeur replied. He helped him out of the car and slowly led him into the penthouse. Once at home, Ruben sank heavily into an easy chair and heaved a deep sigh. "Dear God," he whispered, "I have a feeling that something traumatic is about to happen to me; I have had bad days before, but this is too much."

Why subconsciously did the words "Dear God" come to him? They had never crossed his mind since the day he left Winnipeg. He felt that the words were a bad omen. He had turned away from religion the night he arrived in Vancouver, when, for the second time, he had had to survive in an alien world. God hadn't helped him then, when he desperately needed Him. He had not come to his aid when railway police were chasing him across the tracks. Why should he call upon Him now? In Ruben's opinion, religion and prayer were useless exercises, although to naive persons they might perhaps bring some sort of spiritual comfort.

CHAPTER 10

It was a gloomy morning. The sky was overcast with a dark sea of clouds. A cold wind blew, ruffling the tree tops, and a light rain fell. The traffic was heavy — car horns blared, windshield wipers slapped with the rhythm of a heart beat, and, somewhere above in the depths of the heavy clouds, the drone of an airplane could be heard.

Ruben stood in a corner of his balcony, leaning against a wall, and watched the rain falling slowly, methodically accumulating into puddles. The balcony door slowly slid open and Pierre appeared.

"Would you like to come inside, sir?" he asked deferentially. "It's quite chilly out here."

Ruben agreed and left the balcony for the warmth and comfort of the living room.

"Sit down and talk a bit. You know, Pierre, I have been thinking about what old age actually represents and I have come to the conclusion that aging becomes an increasingly traumatic experience. It is a point in the cycle of life that one reaches when one gets a feeling of abandonment. Old age begins when one sees friends gradually slip away. But it also means becoming mellow, facing reality in mind and spirit." He suddenly changed the subject: "Pierre, do you remember the day I hired you?"

"Of course I do, Mr. Ruben."

"I asked you that day if you would mind if I called you Pierre instead of Peter. That, you will remember, was the name of Miss Helga's chauffeur. He gave such fine service to both Miss Helga and to me that I vowed that if I ever acquired the means to have a chauffeur for myself, I would want to call him by that name. You see, Pierre, the name represents to me continuity in my life. I associate it with my glorious image of the past which will, I hope, preserve wonderful memories of Helga."

"I think I understand".

"I want you to know that I am grateful to you for going along with the change of name", Ruben continued. "You are a most loyal employee too."

As Pierre shuffled his feet in embarrassment and spoke his thanks, Ruben changed the subject. "Tell me, Pierre, have you ever been in love?"

Again Pierre seemed to be embarrassed as he replied, "No, sir, I have never been in love with the opposite sex."

"May I ask why not?"

"Let's just say that I am a simple man with simple desires and love is not one of them. I am over fifty-five years old," Pierre continued, "too old to get involved in a relationship, unless something unexpectedly were to happen in my life that would necessitate a change. At the moment, however, it seems unlikely."

"Do you mean to tell me that you have no desire to make love to a beautiful woman?"

"There are ways of avoiding such love affairs if one knows how."

It was obvious that Pierre was losing his composure by being questioned about such personal matters. "Will that be all, sir?"

"Yes, my friend, that will be all," Ruben replied and let his mind wander back to lovely visions of romantic encounters he had experienced, the memories of which were now buried in the glorious past. Only scanty invisible threads of a deeper significance remained in his mind which he tried to recreate, and perhaps find a purpose worthwhile pursuing. His thoughts flashed further back to the farm, his childhood and, of course, his friends whom he hadn't seen in over half a century and didn't have a clue as to their whereabouts.

The sudden peal of the front door chimes brought Ruben to his senses. He opened the door himself. Standing there was Ingi, tall, handsome, and smiling.

"My dear Ingi," Ruben exclaimed, his voice trembling. "What a wonderful thing to see you again! Why didn't you call me when you got in town?"

"I'm sorry, I didn't mean to startle you. I didn't call first because I wanted to surprise you", Ingi explained.

"Please come in, and sit down", Ruben said, ushering his friend into the living room. "I'm so happy to see you again. I've thought about you many times, yet I hadn't heard from you. How is the car business going?"

"Terrific", Ingi replied. "I'm selling cars by the dozen."

For a moment Ruben's mind wandered back to Stockholm, the Salt johaden and Malaren beaches, and the enjoyable times he had there with Helga and later with Ingi for a short time. "How is your love life?" Ruben asked jokingly.

"Very good, and yours?"

"Mine ended when I lost Helga," he lamented.

"Don't despair, my friend, I'll see what I can do for you while I'm in town."

"Forget it," Ruben replied with a wave of his hand.

He poured drinks for the two of them and continued bringing his friend up to date. "I went to see my doctor yesterday, and in a subtle way he reminded me that I am over sixty and must slow down. He intimated that I can live a relatively normal life as long as I don't enjoy it! I remember the time when I was an idol, a hero, a tycoon and a lover. I had the power to manipulate, put things to use or abuse, days were filled with business meetings and the nights with bliss and the pleasures of love. Now I have to sit back and watch the world go by. My friend, I am just a decaying tooth waiting in pain to fall out.

"I don't know if the screwy story about Adam and Eve that I learned in Hebrew school was in fact the beginning of mortality. According to the history of creation, which in my opinion is no more than a legend, a serpent enticed Eve to eat forbidden fruit from the tree of wisdom. She in turn persuaded Adam to do likewise. As a result of their disobedience, or stupidity, people have been dying ever since. Poor souls, he continued. "Every one of us is totally involved with himself, and, like an ant in the grass, is fighting for survival only to be crushed by a heavy boot in due course."

"You are giving me the impression that you are very lonely, which leads me to a relevant question."

"Please ask me, and I shall be honest with my reply."

"Through the years, were you really a compulsive loner?"

"Yes, my friend, except for Helga, who gave me hope, love and inspiration." He put his hand on Ingi's shoulder and continued, "You see, I was never a self-made hero. Helga made it all happen. As a result others began seeking my friendship in order to gain a small measure of faith for their limited expectations in life. They were forever buzzing around me like insects around a street light on a humid summer night. All they were really seeking was a small measure of hope and security, hanging on to unrealized ambitions, hoping to derive some measure of success by associating with me. I refused to get involved in long-lasting friendships. Life to me then was beautiful music, a trio comprised of sunshine, moonlight and romance which I treasured. I wanted to enjoy my life in freedom rather than pretending to be someone's Messiah. Freedom has always been dear to me. My guiding principle has always been:

Don't walk behind me, I may not lead you;
Don't walk in front of me, I may not follow you;
Just walk beside me and be my friend."

"Who are you quoting?" Ingi asked.

"I think it's Comus," Ruben replied.

"If this is your philosophy, how come you got totally involved with Helga?" his friend wondered.

"I was desperate. I had a feeling that she just might turn out to be my liberator, and she was! I confess that I had an ulterior motive when I first met her. However, with the passage of time I fell hopelessly in love with her. She was an exceptional person and I admired everything about her. Now I feel like I'm suspended in time. One side of me tries to hang on to the past, while the other strives to make me aware of the present. These two forces are responsible for my depressed and confused state of mind."

On the television set was a photograph of a beautiful woman. Ingi studied it for a while and cautiously asked, "Who is this charming creature?"

"Oh, this is my Helga," his friend sadly replied. "My dear beautiful treasure. She was the only person in the world I truly loved!"

"I'm sorry I asked," Ingi muttered apologetically. He glanced at his watch and remarked, "My friend it's quite late. I'd better head for the hotel. Good-night, I'll see you tomorrow," and softly closed the door behind him.

Ruben crawled into bed and after some tossing and turning fell fast asleep. He was terrified by frightening nightmares again but couldn't wake up. Grotesque visions of the past kept appearing in bizarre forms. He had a feeling that he was falling with lightning speed into an abyss. He was flying through space deeper and deeper while frightening objects were flashing by his eyes. He subconsciously raised his arm and hit the lamp on the night table. The loud crash of porcelain woke him up. He sat up, looked around the dark room and staggered over to the window. He pulled the drapes open and saw a dark, misty sky. It was morning. The sky was leaden gray and a fine drizzling rain was falling.

The door chimes rang softly. "Come on in. It's open," Ruben called out. Ingi entered, looked at his friend with deep concern, and said, "You don't look too good today. Don't you feel well?"

"I'm all right considering the horrible nightmares I had most of the night. What time is it?"

"It's eleven o'clock," Ingi replied. "Did I wake you up?"

"Not really. I was not asleep. I was sort of suspended in the twilight zone but couldn't get up. I know you are concerned," Ruben continued, "but please, don't smother me with pity or sympathy. I do that very well by myself."

Although Ingi could see Ruben was tired and moody, he was anxious to talk with him. He wanted to share with him some of the experiences he had in Winnipeg, including his involvement with a girl he had met. "I am bursting to tell you something," Ingi impatiently informed his friend.

"I'm all ears, shoot," Ruben replied.

"I was walking down Main Street a few nights ago and dropped into a bar. I sat down, had a couple of drinks, and was unexpectedly confronted by a gorgeous-looking blond. She very smoothly snuggled up to me and with a sparkle in her green eyes asked, 'What's your name'? 'What's it to you?' I countered. 'Nothing really,' she giggled, 'except you're good looking and a Swede, I presume.' 'What's so special about Swedes?' 'Well,' she hesitated, 'Swedes have a reputation of being good lovers!' I tried to discourage her but she clung to me. Before I knew what was happening, I was in a dark room at the rear, making love to her. It was a long gratifying night, the kind one doesn't easily forget."

"Did she actually seduce you?" Ruben asked laughing.

"Of course not. I agreed to have a go at it, you know? Oh yes, her name is Brigette. She's originally from Norway, although I think she is French."

"It ony proves again that the West is indeed hospitable to all comers," Ruben chuckled. "Are you intending to marry her?"

"You must be kidding!" Ingi emphatically replied. "At first, I figured she was no more than a passing shadow in the night that would disappear the day I leave Winnipeg. But I've been spending every night with Brigette and I'm now getting accustomed to her always being around. I'm thinking of her more and more. However, marriage is just not for me. I'm a professional lover. I deal with the sex-hungry. My motto has always been: 'Love them and leave them!'"

Ingi glanced at his watch and stood up. He was returning to Montreal on an early afternoon flight but would see Ruben again on his next visit. He paused then said, "She has asked me to move to Winnipeg and live with her."

"Are you going to?"

"Not on your life!" Ingi replied. "I don't really love her enought to get my neck into a noose!"

"Good luck, my friend. Give Brigette my best."

Ruben saw Ingi to the door and thought, "Perhaps I'll meet her one day and even have an affair with her myself, if that's possible." He sat down on a sofa and seriously tried to put his present existence into proper perspective. "I'm well aware that grieving will only prolong my lonely days and nights and affect my emotions. I shall try to grieve no more. Instead, I shall make an attempt to fill my heart with simple daily things which might bring some peace to my soul. I must rise, stand tall, and perhaps recapture some of my past dignity."

Ruben was sorry now that he had never married. His compulsive obsession to succeed had driven him all his life to achieve prestige, wealth and power in the world of business. Had he married perhaps he would have had a son to give continuity to his name, thus beating mortality. As it was, only a tomb-stone would remain. Everything else about him would be forgotten as if he had never lived.

Loud ringing of the telephone brought Ruben to reality. He picked it up and shouted, "Hello, who is it?"

"This is Brigette. Ingi left me your number and I promised I would give you a ring once in a while. How are you feeling?"

"I am feeling great!" Ruben replied with a chuckle. "One of these days I would very much like to meet you."

"I would like that too," she replied.

After a brief conversation Ruben insisted, "Please call me again, real soon!"

"I will, I promise. Bye for now," she cooed and hung up.

"She sounds very nice. I must meet her one day soon," he promised himself. "Very few pages are left in my book of life," he thought and remained sitting, gazing at the Persian rug on the floor.

It seemed only a few minutes later when he pulled the drapes open and was surprised to see that it was night outside. The city was ablaze with lights and the stars were obscured by dark clouds. He recalled the cheap saloon he had visited the other night where he almost allowed himself to be seduced. He was sorry he resisted.

"I know it's silly of me to even be thinking about it. I would like to try it even though I doubt my ability to perform, should an opportunity present itself again." A voice inside him kept urging him on, "Go, go to the saloon." He finally decided to satisfy his urge.

Black clouds moved in from all directions, lightning split the sky and deep thunder rolled in the distance. Rain began but it didn't discourage Ruben. He kept plodding toward the whore-house as if he was being pulled by an invisible force.

CHAPTER 11

The saloon was a haven, a shelter from the storm that raged over the city. The shadows of prostitutes lurking in the doorways, along the street, out of the rain, seemed deeper than they had been on his first visit.

He sat down at a table, ordered a cup of coffee, took a sip, and grimaced at the taste.

"What's the matter, big shot? Don't you like our coffee?" the waitress asked.

"It could recharge a rundown truck battery", he shot back.

"If you don't like it, you know where you can go", she snarled.

"I know, I know", Ruben said. "Get me a rye — make it a double."

He nursed the drink, and tried to keep his eyes open. Someone touched his shoulder. He slowly turned around and looked at a face, a face he thought he had seen before. His voice trembling with uncertainty, "What do you want?" Ruben asked.

"My name is Andy", the man replied. "And you must be Finky Finkel!"

Ruben turned white and stammered, "You mean ... you are Andy Posarek?"

"Yes, that's me," the other replied.

"This is incredible!" Ruben exclaimed, "it's impossible ..." His lips were parched, his mouth sand-dry, his hands trembled. The saloon spun and the table he hung on for support appeared tilted. His heart reverberated in his ears.

They fell into each other's arms and wept like children. "How did you recognize me?" Ruben asked, wiping tears away.

"It never entered my mind that I would find you here, or

anywhere for that matter. The minute I sat down your face drew my attention. I thought it was familiar," Andy replied, almost incoherently. "I watched you for a while until I was sure who you were, even though a lifetime has gone by since we last saw each other on the Salter Bridge. You said then 'When the day comes for me to leave this city I swear I'll never return'. Remember?"

"Yes, I remember," Ruben sighed. "But as we grow older we become mellower, we begin yearning to touch the past in order to find some meaning to the present which is so terribly temporary. We try to recapture memories of youth, fantasies and dreams that vanished forever. This is basically why I have returned. I am looking for a place where I can rest my tired head and perhaps find some solitude in the process."

Ruben studied Andy's face. It looked sad. He wondered how life had treated him.

"When did you come to town?" Ruben asked.

"Only a few hours ago", Andy replied.

"What made you come back? Are you planning to settle down here", Ruben inquired, with curiosity in his voice.

"I don't really have an answer to your questions — not just yet, anyway."

Andy's obvious reluctance to talk restrained Ruben from asking what would have been his next, and natural, question — about Esther. Instead, he asked Andy where he was staying in Winnipeg.

"Nowhere just yet", said Andy, uncertainty in his voice.

"In that case, you are most welcome to stay with me for as long as you wish."

"Thank you very much, I'd like that", Andy replied eagerly.

In Ruben's apartment, Andy sank back in with a sigh of contentment in a deeply cushioned chair. In the brief silence, Ruben thought, "It's hard to believe we would meet the way we did tonight — it was just fate, I suppose. I'm not a fatalist because the validity of fate can't be proved. But it does seem that we are definitely children of destiny in one form or another."

Then Ruben broke the silence: "Tell me, Andy, how did my mother react to the way I so suddenly left home?"

"She worried about you for a long time until ...." said Andy.

"Until what?" Ruben asked.

"My mother told me that, with you gone, of course she lived alone in her attic apartment. She became very ill, but no one knew about it. One day my mother dropped in to see her, saw how sick she was and had her taken to the hospital. But it was too late — your mother passed away only a few days later."

"Thank you, my friend."

Ruben wiped a tear from his face, turned to Andy staring at the floor and continued, "I still remember the panic, the sickening fright I had when I was leaving Winnipeg on that unforgettable day. Fear was in my heart and I was doubting the wisdom of my actions but I had no alternative. There was no turning back. I curled up in a corner of an empty box car and tried to divert my mind from what seemed trivial at one time, but had suddenly become painfully important. I was thinking about our gray cat, Minnie, on the farm. She arched her back when agitated or she would rub herself against my leg and purr contentedly. There were many things that tormented my mind when I was finally accomplishing what I wanted for a long time."

The two friends talked until morning, then Ruben stood, stretched and went out on his balcony. The sun was slowly rising from the depths of a fiery horizon and sparkling diamonds of dew covered flower-beds and green grass. The air was invigorating, fresh and pure as if it had just emerged from a clear waterfall. He had seen many cities in his life, but never could afford the time to observe the charm they projected. Here he felt at home. Perhaps the simplicity and innocence of this city made him feel that way. The streets were deserted and a fine haze was rising from the asphalt.

Ruben was captivated by two worlds, the sun rising against a deep luminous blue sky and the world below. White tall buildings were shimmering in the sunlight. Others, built of lumber many years ago, had turned into rusty faded boxes discoloured by time.

The houses were encircled by patches of grass, crowned with shingle roofs in various shapes and colours, just sitting there weeping for the elegance they once projected. The trees, although greenish, appeared tired and wilted as if they were praying for rain to refresh their thirsty leaves.

Andy came out and announced, "There are two of your friends in the living room waiting to see you."

Inside, Ruben found Ingi and a woman sitting on the sofa. They appeared to be highly nervous. "Well, what a pleasant surprise seeing my friend Ingi again. Now I am sure you like our city. You have come back!" exclaimed Ruben.

"Let's just say that my coming back is not by choice."

"What do you mean?"

Ingi ignored his friend's question, stood up, took him aside and whispered, "You probably remember me telling you of meeting a girl on my first visit, her name is..."

Brigette quickly got up and introduced herself. "I am the girl that once called you, remember?"

"Of course I do, I was meaning to call you back, but misplaced your phone number. I am truly sorry. Needless to say, I am very happy to meet you. Ingi here told me all about you, how charming you are, and he was right!"

"Thank you."

Ruben studied her face, her shapely figure and said, "I hope this is the beginning of a lasting friendship."

"I'm sure it is," she replied.

"Oh, I'm sorry," turning to Andy, he continued. "This is my dear childhood friend Andy. We haven't seen each other in over forty-five years. I can't even begin to tell you how happy I am meeting him again."

For a few minutes everyone remained uncomfortably silent, then Andy turned to Brigette and remarked, "Winnipeg is a nice city, isn't it?"

"It certainly is," she agreed, "especially on a hot Sunday afternoon such as this. You can almost hear the deserted streets breathing. Hardly anything is moving except the leaves on the trees."

"It's days like this", Ruben remarked, "that keep reminding me of my youth — much has happened, much has happened."

CHAPTER 12

One June day, when the sun was shining brilliantly, when the clear sky was deep and bluer than blue, when grass and flower beds were drenched with sunshine, Andy and Ingi were sitting on a bench in the shade of a huge tree in Kildonan Park. The river was calm, undisturbed, like a pond of heavy oil basking in the sun.

"What, if I may ask, did you and Ruben discuss yesterday about Brigette?" Andy asked.

"Oh, that," Ingi remarked. "As a matter of fact I have been meaning to tell you the whole story."

"I have always strongly believed that emotional happenings should be shared. It makes it easier on the soul when you get it off your chest, so to speak. We all have accumulated experiences and hidden emotions, but there comes a time when we begin seeking someone with whom we can share our joys, our sorrows, our disappointments in life and unfulfilled aspirations we all have buried deep in our subconscious, including yourself."

"Me? What do you mean?"

"My friend, your face, your indifference to life, is an open book and your eyes are windows to a wounded soul."

"Spare me your philosophy. Let's be honest with each other, perhaps it'll be beneficial to both of us", Andy protested.

"About two months after I had returned to Montreal," Ingi continued, "I received a letter from Brigette informing me that she was pregnant and would I come back to Winnipeg to talk things over. I was feeling guilty. Although I doubted her claim, I nevertheless agreed to see her. Andy, I want you to know that I'm not a novice, nor was I a virgin when I turned fifteen, and to my knowledge, I never made anyone pregnant. However, accidents do happen. I returned to find out the truth. I didn't love her enough to marry her, but I thought, should her story prove to be true, I would be prepared to live with her, even though I had the sickening feeling a noose was slowly tightening around my neck.

"When I arrived in Winnipeg, she met me at the airport, her smile and sparkling, penetrating green eyes welcomed me and overpowered my feelings of resentment. We talked for days. We sat in city parks many nights, when time stood still and soundless melodies slowly began penetrating my emotions. I had a feeling that I was slowly but surely falling in love with Brigette. To this day I don't know what hypnotic power possessed me when I asked her to marry me. She was ecstatically happy to hear those unbelievable words. She hesitated for a minute and answered, 'I thought you would never ask!' We were married soon after.

"The night that followed will forever remain in my memory. 'Ingi, my dear Ingi,' she sighed while caressing me, 'I can't live with a lie and I didn't mean to deceive you. I was desperate and wanted my baby to have a legitimate father. Ingi, you are not my baby's father,' she whispered, while tears rolled down her face. 'I was already pregnant when we had our first affair. I love you very much though, and wanted to see you again."

"'How did you manage to get yourself into such a mess?' Her answer was, 'How can one think of any sort of prevention in a smelly room in the rear of a filthy restaurant? Please understand, I'm not a professional hooker. Life has been cruel to me. I had to find some means of survival and I am hoping that with your help I'll succeed in returning to a respectable, normal life.'"

"And you fell for it, hook, line and sinker!" Andy interjected.

"Not really", Ingi went on. "Brigette pleaded with me, begging me not to be angry, and said she would free me if that's what I wanted. I began to feel compassion for her and I realized there was pity mixed with love in my heart. Even though I now know she had manipulated me, that somehow didn't seem important. I was really and truly beginning to love her. I ignored what she had tried to do to me and thought of her fine qualities. She has one of those rare smiles that gives reassurance. She faces, or seems to face, the whole world for an instant, and then concentrates on you, with an irresistible gleam in your favour. You think you are hearing drums in the distance. They come closer, until your ears begin to throb. I guess that's what you're supposed to feel when you're in love."

"That's your philosophy of love, I suppose", Andy said. "But what finally happened?"

Ingi's face dropped, and in a low voice told Andy that, a few days later, Brigette had been taken to a hospital, where she had a miscarriage.

At Ruben's penthouse later, Andy told his host of the interesting day he had had with Ingi. "Have you seen Brigette?" he inquired. Ruben shook his head, "Why do you ask?" With an air of indifference, Andy said, "I just wondered."

"You know, Andy", said Ruben, "Brigette sometimes arouses strange feelings in me, the kind I haven't had since I lost Helga. I have a shameless urge to have an affair with her when the opportunity comes."

"You are not the only one", Andy commented, at the same time wondering if at some time he might be attracted to her.

"Now, my old friend, the time has come to talk about something else", Ruben said firmly. "You have been talking with Ingi and with me about Brigette, a woman you have just met, and you haven't said a word about your wife. Why is Esther not with you? Where *is* Esther?"

Andy shook his head. "I wish I knew where she is", he said sadly.

CHAPTER 13

"It all began the day the doctor told me I was sterile. Esther desperately wanted a child and that traumatic news made her irritable and quarrelsome. I suggested adopting a baby but she wouldn't hear of it. She kept avoiding me, yet often reassured me that she was not disappointed.

"During our last few years together, Esther's guilt for disobeying her father increasingly occupied her thoughts until she realized that she had abandoned everything she loved dearly and was making a futile attempt to adjust to a lifestyle that still remained foreign to her. She found it impossible to free herself from the guilt that was constantly tormenting her soul. She found herself yearning for her family home, her parents, her brother and the orthodox way of life she had given up. She had been brought up in a Chassidic home. She craved the sanctity that prevailed on Friday evenings when her mother would light the Sabbath candles and her father and Bernie would walk together to the Synagogue. It seemed as though a spiritual light shone from her father's eyes then.

"As the memories of her childhood plagued her, Esther successfully hid her true feelings from me. Time, however, began taking its toll. She became more pale and thinner. Her interest in me and life in general was diminishing. Her indifference had all the signals for me to notice her unhappiness but I failed her, failed to realize how much she was silently suffering.

"She slowly began to grow away from me, especially since she had been told that she would never have the good fortune of raising a family. Finally, in desperation, she decided to leave me, even though I know she loved me passionately. She wrote me a note one day, walked out and never returned.

*Dear Andy, You know how deep my love is for you, and
yet, for the last few years I have been
yearning for something, I couldn't understand. My father's words, "Esther, it'll
never work" have been haunting me. I have
finally decided to leave you. Please don't
try to find me, just live with the knowledge
that I love you now and always will. Good luck
and God bless you. Thank you for the many
years you have shared with me.*

Esther.

"I sat at the kitchen table," Andy continued, "a paralyzing feeling permeated my body. I was unable to comprehend the message. I was aware that Esther was unhappy, but had never expected her to suddenly leave. Joys throughout the years, which were many, were racing through my mind with unbelievable clarity and the agonizing years I had lived through trying to get her parents' permission.

"We laughed together, we cried together, but always kissed and made up. What am I to do?

"I sat there till dawn broke. I got up and stumbled out of the apartment. I looked up to the Heavens and silently prayed, 'God, grant me serenity to accept the things I cannot change and strength to endure this horrible sorrow!' I wandered aimlessly, all day, and by nightfall returned home, hoping that Esther might call. I saw her in my mind's eye, her angelic face, her velvety voice whispering, 'I love you.' The compassionate look in her eyes, her beautiful mouth, her sensuous lips, her soft hands caressing my face, that soothed my soul in times of sadness. I sat for months near the phone hoping that she would eventually call. With the passage of time, however, my hope gradually died and I surrendered to cruel reality.

"Loneliness revealed to me that, beyond the first pangs of despair, anguish and grief, I had to find a key to a deeper insight if I was to survive. I sought the courage to go on living but had a frightening feeling that I would not succeed. I became angry with God.

'Can you not divert your attention elsewhere, rather than persecute me?' I shouted at Him. He was silent.

"Over the years I hung onto the faint hope of finding Esther one day. My grief and longing intensified as each 'tomorrow' became 'today'. At night, when I passed out with exhaustion, I would dream of her. She would smile and caress my face. She would tell me how terribly sorry she was. I would then reach out to touch her, to embrace her and tell her how much I loved her, only to discover she was never there. The dreams haunted me. I became desperate, hovering on the brink of insanity.

"I packed a few personal belongings and left Montreal. I wandered from one country to another but the more I tried to escape from myself, the greater my sorrow.

"I ended up in Tel Aviv, holed up in a seedy hotel near Ben Gurion airport. I slept for days, then went for a walk and boarded a bus which took me some distance out of the city. I wandered through fragrant orange groves, and fascinatingly beautiful desert flowers, some growing out of cracks in granite rocks. The effect of the desert was almost hypnotic and it calmed me.

"I remembered Esther saying, 'Andy, why don't we plan on visiting Israel in the near future. I have a distinct feeling that such a tour would bring us closer to God.'

"I was there alone. Why? What was I doing there?

"But I knew that if I were to remain, that enchanting land would hold me, cling to me. The sand, the stones and the mountains would silently speak to me and capture my heart.

"A few days later I began looking for a job. After several fruitless attempts, I managed to get a part-time job driving a cab. I was assigned to the old district in and around Jerusalem. Every Friday when the sun dipped into the captivating rainbow coloured reflections of the distant horizon, I parked on a side street and joined hundreds of Chassidic Jews coming in droves to the Western Wall to welcome the Sabbath with prayer, song and dance.

"The vacant courtyard would swiftly fill up with Chassidim and religious chanting from hundreds of throats would reverberate against the Holy Wall, echoing through old narrow streets nearby. A Divine presence hovered over them, as they praised and thanked God for protecting them and assisting them in living through another week. The chanting seemed to make centuries melt away. I mingled with the crowd, learning more about the Jewish religion and traditions which I proudly and willingly accepted.

"On occasion, when there was no one around. I would enter the courtyard. The silence was mesmerizing.

"The Western Wall, I learned, formed the remains of a once holy temple. I liked the silent lament of this ruin that attested to the martyrdom of a grief-stricken nation. I also frequently visited Mount Zion, over which it is believed, angels are forever hovering. It was hypnotic, listening to imaginary voices singing, drifting in the desert wind, reverberating against the majestic hills of Judea in the distant transparent haze. Even though part of me felt it was no more than hallucination, it nevertheless helped calm me. Such and similar experiences seemed to bring a bit of serenity to my soul.

I found myself involved with orthodox groups and each morning, I would park my cab on the street and join the Chassidim in worship at a small old synagogue, where I hoped to find some consolation for my troubled emotions. I learned to pray with total devotion by reciting the prayers aloud as the Chassidim did.

And thou shalt love the Lord thy
God with all thine heart, and with
all thy soul, and with all thy
might ...

"I learned the full meaning of Chassidic religion and the piety such Jews practice in their daily lives, as compared with my own life. Thus the nature of Esther's background became clearer to me. Esther grew up in a Chassidic home under the influence of her parents, who lived according to the laws of the *Torah*, traditions, rituals, customs and total dedication to Chassidic morality.

"I had thought that converting to Judaism would keep us together, but conversion was not enough to bridge the gap that existed between our cultures. Separation was inevitable.

"However, instead of despairing, I continued to read on Chassidicism and began to understand the true meaning of the word 'Chassid.' A Chassid, I learned, is an ultra-pious Jew, whose entire life is dedicated to God with prayer as the integral core of his existence. A Chassid is also a disciple of a great pious Rabbi, a follower of the unique Chassidic philosophy and the prescribed pious way of life. Such an individual tries to obey with grace and humility all aspects of religious morality, which is a part of the 613 *Torah* (Laws) commandments and statutes to which a Chassid is obligated throughout his life and feels privileged in serving God.

"The Chassidic movement was founded in the 18th century, by a man who was a mystic and a poet. His name was Israel ben (son of) Eliezer. He preached in simple language to simple people. He was a visionary who thrived on expression, compassion and charity. His influence raced throughout central and eastern Europe, where Jews had been subjected for centuries to pogroms, oppression and persecution. They eagerly accepted his message that brought new hope into their lives. It offered them for the first time hope to achieve unity with God and a purpose in life, and attracted thousands of Jews all over the world.

"An entire new culture within a culture grew up around the liberating vision. He rejuvenated the Jews, their hopes and their aspirations. They were infused with a Divine spirit which made them capable of dealing with anti-Semitism, poverty, and accepting adversity without sensitivity.

"It also offered Jews a new kind of communion that would hopefully bring them redemption and salvation. That is one of the reasons why lighting the Sabbath candles on Friday at sun-down is one of the most satisfying spiritual experiences one can possibly attain. The candles create a divine holiness and bring sanctity into the home. It is a bond that unites families unlike any other tradition.

"A poem by Spinoza expresses the joy and feeling of sanctity in a home that practices the lighting of Sabbath candles. These few lines from the poem set out the beauty and the importance of the ritual:

Thou beautiful Sabbath, thou sanctified day,
That chasest our cares and our sorrows away.

O come with good fortune, with joy and with peace,
To the homes of thy pious, their bliss to increase!

In honour of thee are the tables decked white;
From the clear candelabra shines many a light;

All men in the finest of garments are dressed,
As far as his purse each hath got him the best.

"Chassidim all over the world continues to thrive on this culture to this day."

"After a few years in Israel, I became restless again and decided to move on — this time, to Holland. I found it to be a city full of antiquities, spotlessly clean, and unique. Despite the legalization of bawdy houses, most of which were concentrated in one section of the city, I discovered there was less incidence of rape and fewer sex offenders than in a comparable city in North America. I was reminded of a proverb: 'Forbidden fruit is always more inviting and sought after.' Around me bright clean buildings stood proudly, gleaming in sunshine near and around the many canals, projecting serenity and pride."

"I continued to explore Judaism. I read the *Diary of Anne Frank* and was moved by the sight of the hiding place that was her refuge. It was in a very narrow building in the middle of a block of identical, attached structures. An extremely narrow winding stairway led to the hiding place, at the very top. On the walls, downstairs, were countless resoutions, adopted by the United Nations over many years, but never implemented. They were useless, meaningless pieces of paper, wrinkled and discoloured by time."

"I came upon a synagogue, built by Portuguese and Spanish Jews more than three hundred years ago. From the historical records which I saw in that synagogue, I learned that, despite the heroic efforts and sacrifices of the Dutch people, the rest of the world pretended not to be aware of the darkest days in the annals of history. I was horrified to hear that, because of Nazi genocide, only twelve thousand Jews then lived in Amsterdam.

"Life in Amsterdam was free and easy, discrimination was almost non-existent, and I felt that I was in a true democracy. Like Heinrich Heine, the German poet, I was deeply impressed by the easy style of life in Amsterdam. I agreed with Heine that 'When the end of the world is about to come, I'll go to Amsterdam, where everything happens fifty years later'."

"But the pull on my Canadian roots was strong and I returned to Winnipeg."

Ruben sat beside Andy, "You're home now, my friend," he said.

Andy lay his head on Ruben's shoulder. His story had exhausted him and he closed his eyes and slept like a baby.

CHAPTER 14

The first rays of sunlight were just breaking through the slowly departing clouds of night. Ruben had left Andy on the couch and was surprised now to find it empty.

"Andy?"

"In here!" Andy replied from the kitchen. Ruben found him staring out the window.

"Why the long face?" Ruben asked

"I'm just thinking about my terrible loss."

"You mean Esther?"

"Yes, of course."

"But that happened over thirty years ago!"

"I know. But when I sit alone, with no one to talk to, the whole thing comes back to me, in my mind, again and again. It's as though it had only happened yesterday."

Andy looked at Ruben and implored:

"Tell me — how can I free myself from that awful feeling of guilt that I have? It keeps clawing at me, at my brain. I should have known she needed help, she was so very unhappy, but I took her for granted. Why am I feeling guilty? Because I failed her. I was living in my own happiness and I thought that she too was happy. I never gave it a serious thought even when her behaviour sometimes seemed a bit strange and she wouldn't tell me what was wrong. She just didn't confide in me. I think she was preparing, getting ready for the day to destroy us both."

Ruben made some coffee. He poured a cup for each of them, then sat down.

"I think that each one of us has a story" Ruben said, "a story of guilt, buried deep down inside. We think that our grief, the anguish we feel from the guilt, is unbearable. To us, it is

108

unbearable. However, Andy, remember that we are all caught up in the scheme of life and, as the years go by, we realize and understand more clearly how some traumatic episodes came into our lives. But by the time we understand how they occurred, it's too late to correct them.

"It's been fifty years since my only brother was killed and I still live with a horrible feeling of sorrow. When that happened, my father cut off all relationships with me, with my mother and, I sometimes think, with the entire human race. I have thought about that tragedy on many sleepless nights through the years and I have come to one conclusion. I am convinced that my father's indifference to me and my future had a serious effect. I know his apathy also made my mother turn away from me and think only of herself and her sorrow. That whole event, and especially my father's attitude, had a profound influence on my thinking, my sense of values, and subsequently my destiny."

The sun that welcomed Ruben earlier in the day had vanished behind gloomy clouds. A morning shower was dampening the street below.

"Let's go for a walk", Ruben suggested. "Perhaps that will divert our thoughts to more cheerful directions."

"But it's raining", his friend protested.

"So what? I wish I had the nerve to walk barefoot on Portage Avenue the way Helga and I used to walk on the sandy beaches. That would do my heart good!"

They had their walk, despite the rain, and were cheered by it. That night the moon and stars shone in the crystal-clear blue sky and the city was ablaze with lights in the hot humid air. Andy, however, was quite comfortable in Ruben's penthouse, where it was crisp and cool. He was resting in the living room alone. The door chimes rang. He opened the door. It was Brigette.

"I'm sorry to be disturbing you at this hour. It's terribly hot and humid in my apartment, would you mind if I visited for a while?"

"Not at all," Andy replied. "Come in, please and make yourself comfortable. Ruben is out for the evening. I was beginning to feel sort of lonely."

"I know what you mean," Brigette remarked.

"How's Ingi?" Andy asked curiously.

"I don't see him very much at all ..." she said, then changed the subject. "Will you ever stop feeling sorry for yourself?" she asked.

"I didn't know it showed," Andy laughed.

"It certainly does," she continued. "You have wasted most of your life pining for something that is no longer here."

"You mean Esther?"

"Yes, that's who I mean. It's about time you forgot the irretrievable past and for a few years add some meaning to your existence."

"Brigette, are you trying to be another Florence Nightingale?"

"Not really, I merely want to help you join the human race again and make you aware of how little you have accomplished with your noble sacrifice. There comes a time when virtue is no longer a prestigious quality, but rather an unworthy stupidity."

"I don't mean to be rude," Andy replied, "I must say, however, that you don't seem to understand how horrible and meaningless my life has been. You are a young charming woman. Life to you is still a dream to be fulfilled, whereas to me it's a continuous nightmare!"

Caressing his lined face, she moved closer to him. "You are wrong, I do understand!" she whispered, and began to hum softly in his ear.

She placed her hand on his shoulder and continued, "I know it's not easy to hide grief that's carved into one's soul. Even your smile projects some sort of tragic secrecy. 'What's gone and what's past help should be past grief'".

"Yeh," Andy replied with a sigh, "it's easier to preach than to practice. Grief is something one can never overcome. In fact, with the passage of time it gets harder to cope with it. How could I possibly forget the years when Esther and I met secretly, promising love and devotion to one another for ever and ever? We were dreaming beautiful dreams that would one day come true. Now, my heart's shattered beyond repair and my life lost its meaning many years ago with only fragments of memories to justify my existence."

"Andy, what I am about to ask you may sound bold and undignified on my part, but as a friend, I hope you'll be honest with me."

"What would you like to know?" he asked.

"Have you slept with anyone since Esther's disappearance?"

"It never even entered my mind."

"Are you impotent?" she pressed on.

"No, but I couldn't father a child. Esther desperately wanted to have children."

She cupped his face gently with both hands, kissed him, and asked, "Andy, do you like me?"

"Brigette, please, I really don't appreciate being cross-examined about intimate matters!"

"I'm sorry," Brigette cooed, "I want to help."

"Don't bother, I like it where I am," he countered. Andy suddenly began feeling warm, perspiration appeared on his forehead. A long forgotten sensation crept up his spine. Passion that lay dormant for over thirty years stirred and ignited a spark that threatened to explode into a flame. It was strange to him, but his resistance was crumbling.

"Please, Brigette, if you are as good a friend as you claim to be, don't tempt me; it would be criminal for me to even entertain the idea of going to bed with you or anyone else, after thirty or more years. I couldn't live with my conscience if I were to succumb to such an immoral act!"

Brigette moved closer to Andy and continued with deep sympathy, "Poor, poor old lovable fool".

"Why are you saying that?" Andy questioned her, some anger in his voice.

"Because only a total idiot would hang on to an impossible dream, hoping to find his wife after she cruelly and thoughtlessly abandoned him over three decades ago."

Andy, slapped her. Brigette recoiled.

"I am sorry", she said, "I shouldn't have said that."

Andy dropped to his knees.

"Brigette, I am sorry, please forgive me. I didn't mean to slap you. I don't know what came over me. I swear it'll never happen again."

Brigette cuddled up to him, like a kitten, and whispered, "I love you, Andy and would like to help you if you will let me." Andy capitulated.

Repressed sexual urges boiled within him. He pulled her dress off, then stopped suddenly.

"Whats the matter darling?" Brigette asked.

"How about Ingi?"

"Don't worry about him, I have a distinct feeling that he is involved with his thrill-seeker friends."

"What makes you think so?"

"I saw him."

Although Andy was trying to resist, he realized he was yielding to Brigette's demands. "Would you like another drink?" she asked sweetly.

"Yes, of course, what the hell, might as well!"

Brigette, by now dressed only in a short transparent slip, walked over to the bar to pour a couple of drinks. "How mature she is, how boldly she stands, half-naked, without a trace of embarrassment! What a figure! I hope I don't disappoint her when the time comes," he thought. Confronted with this situation, overcome by an uncontrollable desire, Andy surrendered to her demands.

"I wish this moment could last until the end of time," she whispered.

"I can feel your heart beat like a hammer against my breasts!" she exclaimed, while exploring his hot quivering body. They were lost in each other's arms and time ceased to exist.

The next morning, Andy awoke very early. He turned on his side, on one elbow. Brigette was lying on her back, sound asleep, hands folded under her head, her breasts exposed. Andy looked around the room. Two empty glasses on the bedside table reminded him of what had happened. Since Esther had vanished he had never had any desire for sex and now, Brigette had changed that overnight.

'I'll never forgive myself," he thought, "I betrayed Esther."

Andy shuffled over to the window, parted the drapes a little, and peered out. It was still early and the city was enveloped in misty, semi-dark tranquility. The pale rays of the rising sun were touching the tops of the tall buildings, night was gradually giving way to dawn. A ray of sunlight reached a corner of the window not covered by the drapes, splashing a glorious reflection on the bedroom carpet.

Brigette stirred, sighed deeply, opened her eyes. "What time is it?"

"Six o'clock," he replied without looking at her.

"My dear boy," she continued, "why are you up so early?"

"I couldn't sleep. I feel very guilty and my conscience is gnawing at me."

"Didn't you enjoy the night with me?"

"Of course I did, but I should never have allowed this to happen."

"You talk like a priest," she laughingly remarked as she raised herself to a sitting position.

"A man my age and my past ought to know better!" He suddenly took hold of her arms and demanded to know, "Do you do this with everyone?"

"I would be dishonest if I were to tell you that you were the first one."

"Oh, I know you are not a virgin," Andy interjected.

"Let me finish", she insisted. "I am not a professional whore, if that's what you mean. However, I have been compelled on rare occasions to engage in repugnant sex play in order to survive. It kept me going while I was seeking ways and means to find some sort of security."

"Didn't you find it by marrying Ingi?"

"Not really. He has his moments, but he is leaning towards homosexuality most of the time, and that frightens me!"

"Brigette, I am not against sexuality in general," Andy remarked in a serious tone. "I am merely saying that sexual relationships can be most gratifying to those whose love and respect are in harmony with each other."

"Are you implying that you don't respect me?"

"No, I respect you," he quickly reassured her, "I am simply trying to say that since Esther's disappearance, I have forgotten the meaning of love and happiness. I'll never stop loving Esther. I keep hearing her soothing voice in the wind and seeing her angelic face in the darkest shadows. I'll never give up searching for her, even though the chances of finding her are next to impossible. I'll never give up hope."

"My darling Andy, I admire you and feel sorry for you at the same time after what you have just said. There is, however, no harm in enjoying to some measure the things life has to offer. You should feel no remorse. You were overdue. It may well be that last night was a new beginning for you."

"I doubt it," Andy replied.

"Would you be a dear and walk me home?"

"I will if you promise me not to ever manipulate me into a repeat performance!"

"I promise," Brigette replied. "From now on, I'll leave it all up to you!"

They walked briskly in the crisp early morning — Brigette, with high hopes and anticipation; Andy, with a solemn promise in his heart never to allow such an act to happen again.

When he returned to the penthouse, he sat on the balcony hearing voices from the past. He remembered the last conversation he had with Esther on a rainy evening in their flat in Montreal.

"My dear Esther," he pleaded, "don't you remember your promise?"

"What promise?" she asked.

"You promised you would love me even when we were old and gray. We aren't even old, we are only beginning." He walked up to her, embraced her and continued, "Don't you remember?"

Esther lifted her head, focused her sad eyes on him and with a deep sigh replied, "I remember. How can I forget it? The night was warm, the air crisp, the moon was full and the heavens were singing a song for us. We thought that nothing would ever change, but changes are forever taking place. Something inside me is slowly dying. I believe destiny has something to do with it."

"What is destiny? It is that influence that takes control of life."

Andy looked into her eyes and asked, "Esther, are you sorry you married me?"

"Every passing day I find it more and more difficult to cope."

"Don't talk like that. I love you."

"I know," she signed, "I love you too. That's what makes it more painful!"

CHAPTER 15

One hot afternoon in July, Ruben saw a crowd and people were buzzing around the Holiday Inn. The air was sticky with heat. Ruben decided to escape to the cool of the hotel lobby. There was a throng of youngsters there attending the Western Junior Music Festival. Young musicians came from all parts of western Canada to compete annually.

Ruben bought a newspaper, and sat down in the crowded lobby. A few feet away was an aging, gray-haired man, chewing on a fat cigar. Ruben's attention was drawn to his neighbour by the latter's clothes. He wore a wide-brimmed Stetson, red and white plaid shirt, high boots. The man's face reminded Ruben of someone he might have met in his travels of the distant past. The face somehow appeared to be familiar, yet Ruben could not identify it. He brushed off the matter as of little importance, and turned to his newspaper.

His curiosity got the better of him, however, and he raised his eyes again, only to become aware that the other man was staring at him, too. Ruben smiled and said, "I get the impression that you're a Westerner."

"Yep, I am — I'm from Edmonton", the other replied.

"What brings you to Winnipeg?"

"Years ago I used to travel from coast to coast with my son to various musical festivals. Michael was a gifted violinist and every year he won top awards. Even though he's no longer with me, I still like to attend competitions like this one in Winnipeg."

"What do you mean — he's no longer with you," Ruben asked.

"Michael is dead — he passed away some years ago", the other replied, his eyes edged with tears.

"I'm very sorry," Ruben said. He shook hands with the man and left the hotel, thinking that he should not have been so inquisitive. On the street he thought, "How stupid of me! I never even asked him his name."

The incident bothered him for the rest of the day. He now felt sure he had met the man before, but he just could not think of his name. He also had an intuition that the stranger would reappear, sometime, somewhere. There was something strange about that unexpected meeting. The subject still worried Ruben when, after taking a sleeping pill, he finally went to bed.

Early the next morning, Ruben's telephone rang steadily, but he was not in the mood to answer it. He glanced at his watch — it was seven o'clock. "What idiot would have the audacity to call at this hour on a Sunday morning", he thought. But the telephone kept ringing every few minutes until, finally, he picked up the receiver and shouted, "Who is this, and what do you want? Do you know what time it is, or don't you own a watch?"

A voice at the other end said something indecipherable to Ruben, who demanded that the caller speak up. The voice became clear:

"We met yesterday in the lobby of the Holiday Inn. I'm from Edmonton, remember? While we were talking I had the feeling we had known each other before, but I didn't like to say anything because I didn't want to seem silly. After you left I began to wonder if you just might be someone I knew well when we were boys together. I haven't seen him for over forty years. His name is Finkel."

Ruben was startled, even a little suspicious.

"That's my name," he said. "But there are a lot of Finkels in Winnipeg. Why did you call me?"

"I was up most of the night trying to find the right Finkel. As you said, there are a lot in Winnipeg and a lot in the phone book. I may have found the right one. I hope so! Are you Ruben Finkel — I mean the one I'm looking for?"

"Why do you want to know?" he asked. "How am I supposed to know which Ruben Finkel you're trying to locate?"

"Does the name Bernie Appleman ring a bell with you?" the caller said.

"Yes, I know the name", Ruben replied. "But just as there are a lot of Finkels, there may well be a lot of Applemans. How do I know that you're the Bernie Appleman I once knew?"

"Did you ever live on a farm in Saskatchewan?" the caller asked.

"Yes, a thousand years ago."

"How about forty or more years ago?"

Ruben remained silent, listening to what the other had to say. The voice went on:

"In that case, you certainly must remember the names of some of your childhood friends!"

"Who are you anyway?" Ruben demanded,

"I am Bernie Appleman", the voice said firmly. "You must remember my sister Esther, our friend Andy, the gophers in the pasture, and you can't have forgotten the Salter Bridge."

"Hold it, please," Ruben interjected. "You *are* the man I met and talked to in the hotel yesterday?"

"Yes, indeed I am", came the reply, with obvious relief. "My friend Finky, at long last I have found you!"

"Bernie, Bernie .... listen to me, Bernie", cried Ruben. "I was sure it was you as soon as you said 'Finky', because only my oldest friends call me that now. Come over as fast as you can. You must make it soon, before I have a heart attack!"

"I'll be there in a few minutes", was the reply. "I have your address from the phone book."

Ruben, almost stunned by the sudden course of events, paced the floor of the living room, over and over again, until at last the door chimes rang. He flung open the door, and there was Bernie, the man in Western garb he had chatted with yesterday. They fell into each other's arms, crying like children.

"Bernie, step back so that I can have a good look at you", Ruben asked. "Bernie ....Bernie ....In more than forty years and several times around the world, I don't think I have met anyone with such a beautiful name."

After the excitement had subsided and the faces wiped dry of tears Ruben urged his friend to sit down beside him, while he searched his confused mind for something to say. "You haven't changed a bit since yesterday", he laughed. "You haven't either", Bernie countered, and they looked at each other, their faces lit up with happiness.

After a separation of more than forty years, there was much to say and there were awkward, even painful, silences. After one lengthy period in which neither spoke, Ruben asked, "Do you still chase girls the way you used to, or have you surrendered to old age as I have?" Immediately he regretted asking such a foolish question, but his senses had become numb and he had been unable to think of anything else to say.

"My friend", Bernie responded, "you say 'chasing girls'. I must tell you I wouldn't know what to do if I caught one!"

"I know what you mean," Ruben agreed.

It was not until late that evening that the reunited friends parted, after exhausting their store of reminiscences. As soon as Bernie had left for his hotel, Ruben called Pierre and instructed him to arrange a party for the following night in the penthouse. Pierre was to see that Andy, Ingi and Brigette were invited.

"A party for whom?" queried Andy when Pierre gave him the invitation.

"Sir, I have not been told", Pierre said. Ruben also dodged the question.

The next evening was clear and warm and, when night fell, the moon and stars shimmered brightly in the crystal sky. The penthouse rooms, ablaze with lights, captivated the guests. Andy, Ingi and Brigette wondered nervously what the surprise would be. When the chimes rang at last, Andy rushed to open the door and turned white at what he saw. There before him was a face he was sure was Bernie Appleman's, yet could it be? He rubbed his eyes with the back of his hand, squinted, and stammered, "Bernie, is that you? My God, it *is* you!"

"Sure it's me. Who did you think it was — Moses? Didn't Finky — I mean Ruben — tell you how we met yesterday?"

"No, he didn't. All he said was that he had a surprise for me."

Now, after forty years apart, the childhood friends — now elderly men — faced each other. Three of the four who had their beginnings on Saskatchewan farms and who represented more than a century of history were together again, re-united in a remarkable way. Later, when their knees stopped trembling and their emotions had quieted, Ruben introduced Brigette and Ingi to Bernie. "If it had not been for these wonderful friends, life wouldn't have been worth living", he said. Brigette squeezed Bernie's hands and said, with a soft laugh, "Don't you believe him, he's putting you on."

They all sat down and Bernie became the centre of attention.

"How has life been treating you, Bernie?" Andy inquired.

"Fair in some ways, cruel in others. About a year after you and Esther left Winnipeg, my mother and father were killed — they lost their lives in a car accident. That's when I decided to leave Winnipeg. I used the Salter Bridge, as Ruben did, as the starting point of my freight train journey West, and managed to reach Edmonton. About a year later I married a very beautiful but simple girl named Rachel, and do you know what?"

"What?" they all perked up their ears.

"She was a virgin!"

"Big deal," interjected Ruben, "During the prime of my life I had virgins, sex hungry professional hookers, peasant girls, nobility — you name it, I've had them all! I always liked variety."

"Isn't it against the Jewish religion to have affairs with non-Jewish women?" Ingi asked, a smirk on his face.

"You should know better than to ask such a silly question," Ruben replied angrily. "Helga wasn't Jewish, and besides, I have never claimed to be religious! I only somewhat related to traditional values over the years. Religion hasn't really touched me since my father passed away."

"Have you ever experienced some sort of prejudice in the

business world?" Ingi asked pointedly. "Why do you ask?" Ruben snapped back.

Ingi seemed uncomfortable about the question, and wiped perspiration off his face.

"My friend," Ruben continued, "I know why you asked that question. It's because I'm Jewish. The answer is no! I never denied being Jewish. I was born into Judaism. I am circumcised as are many non-Jews. Any *Shmuck* can get circumcised. However, it takes a hell of a lot more than that to be Jewish! We in the business world were never concerned about one's religion or nationality. One could be a Chinese, Indian, Japanese, a Turk or a Jew. It's not important who you are but rather what you are!"

It was obvious that Ruben was quite upset. "Ingi," he continued, "just because you are a Swede, and your occupation as a pimp is not quite prestigious, doesn't necessarily reflect a stigma against all Swedes. I strongly believe in religious democracy which makes it possible for everyone to act according to one's own conscience without guilt. I even remember standing in line with non-Jews waiting for my turn to grab some sexual gratification for a few minutes at fifty cents a shot!"

"Was there something specific that brought decay into your religious thinking?" Brigette asked curiously.

"My feelings about religion were greatly affected in a short period of time after I left this city. I had no choice but to surrender to a weird world and strange customs. I have also gained my freedom in the process. I realize now, of course, that I had probably abused it."

Brigette reached for Ruben's hand, gave it a squeeze and said, "We must go now, it's been a long evening and we are all tired. We shall see you all tomorrow." She took Ingi by the arm, said good night and walked out. Bernie also excused himself and left, promising to return in the morning.

Deep in thought, Andy remained sitting, staring at the floor. He said to himself: "Brigette is a charming woman, I like her, even though she manipulated me into an unforgivable act. She is pretending that she loves Ingi, but I remember what she said to me about him the other night. She is also trying to entice Ruben into having an affair with her, which shouldn't be too difficult."

Ruben was pacing the living room thinking: "How wonderful it must feel to have someone to go home with, or come home to. I envy Ingi. He has Brigette."

On the way home, Ingi was the first to speak. "You know Brigette, I feel sorry for Ruben. With Helga's help he obviously succeeded in the business world but he unfortunately lost his identity in the process."

"Yes," Brigette replied. "Money can buy the carnival of life. Money is magic and prestige. It contributes greatly to one's importance and Ruben is no exception."

"You sound as if you have a soft spot in your heart for him," Ingi remarked, a tinge of jealousy in his voice.

"I certainly do, in spite of his constant boasting about his glorious past and lamentations about his present condition. I find him quite interesting, and imposing, too. Don't you?"

"Let's just say that I'm grateful for what he has done for me," Ingi replied, obviously irritated.

The penthouse was quiet and the lights were dimmed. Ruben sat in his bedroom, holding a drink in his hands. He was startled by a soft knock on the door. "Who is it?" he asked.

"It's me, Andy."

"Come in. Will you join me in a drink?"

"Yes, thanks."

"How come you're not yet asleep?"

"I could ask you the same question!" Andy replied.

"Well, let me share something with you."

"What about?"

"Every time I see Brigette I become aroused and would like to try making love to her," Ruben confided in Andy. "Is this normal at my age?"

"Knowing you, I think it is." Andy replied. "You were never the kind of guy who believed that storks delivered babies, although you apparently had an exciting life. You're far from burnt out, I could tell what you are thinking by the way you keep looking at her every time she comes over. What about Ingi?" Andy asked.

"Ingi ....?" Ruben burst into laughter and dismissed the question with a wave of his hand. "He's become a playboy again."

"How do you know?" Andy inquired. "I've been told by a mutual acquaintance. He's a pimp," Ruben said.

"Just wait for an opportunity. It will come — just be patient". As he rose to leave, Andy added, "Good night, Finky."

"Don't you ever call me Finky again!" was Ruben's vigorous response, and he threw a slipper in the direction of Andy as his friend departed. Andy, chuckling to himself, slammed his bedroom door shut.

That night Ruben had a dream. He was in bed with a woman in Laura's room in Vancouver, but it was not Laura, it was Brigette.

"Please, please — hold me tight", Brigette was whispering as she caressed him. Ruben embraced her passionately, and then he reached paradise. Brigette said she wanted to leave Ingi, because she no longer loved him. He no longer seemed to have any interest in her and he ignored her — "because, I am sure, he is involved with pimps and thrill-seekers again."

At the break of dawn Ruben awoke, feeling rejuvenated. On the balcony he breathed in deeply the fresh, crisp morning air. He rang for Pierre, but there was no response.

"I wonder what's come over him?" thought Ruben. "In the last few weeks he hasn't been as immaculate in his appearance and not as punctual as he used to be. There's something bothering him and I wish I knew what it was."

Later that day Bernie called to say his farewells to Ruben and Andy: he had decided to go home. The second parting of such old friends verged on the emotional — all were upset.

After he had gone, Ruben, looking at Andy, thought back to the time, forty odd years ago, when he had told him, while they were on the Salter Bridge, of his yearnings.

"One day soon, I'll spread my wings and I'll fly away like an eagle in search of distant horizons."

Memories that had been almost forgotten raced through his brain in disarray. There was that tragic day on the farm where it all began, as though it had happened only yesterday. In his mind's eye was his older brother Milton whose sudden death had had such dire effects on their parents. There were flashbacks of the good friends, who had problems, too. Everything was so clear in his mind — all he had to do was to stretch out his hand and touch them.

"Perhaps", Ruben thought, "It's not too late to revaluate my life — what's left of it — and put it into the right perspective. But I must have help to do this, and fortunately I have good and old friends I can turn to."

Casting back in his mind the recollections of his friends' fortunes and misfortunes, Ruben thought especially of the one who so recently had said goodbye: "I wonder how Bernie will make out back in Edmonton?"

CHAPTER 16

Since Bernie didn't like flying, he took the train home to Edmonton. Relaxing in his seat, he reflected on the incredible coincidental meeting of his friends, and recreated in his mind's eye the day he left Winnipeg and the events that followed. He visualized how the railway guards relentlessly chased homeless drifters riding freight trains, seeking jobs in distant cities, and how he was one of them, hoping to find a new beginning in a new world. He clearly remembered the day he arrived in Edmonton, so long ago. He walked the streets in all directions, carrying his possessions: $35.00 and a shirt stuffed in a paper bag. There were "For Sale" signs on every other house. He came upon a quiet humble looking street where rows and rows of discoloured, dilapidated clapboard houses were dozing in the shade of huge trees. On a window he noticed a sign, "Room for Rent". He knocked on the door and a woman appeared.

"Vat you vant, and vere from are you?" she asked, wiping her face with a soiled apron.

"I'm from Winnipeg and I need a room," he replied.

"You're Jewish, no?"

"Yes, I am."

"For fifteen dollars a month I'll give you the room and meals too. I am a good cook," she added.

"Fine, I'll take it," Bernie replied. He had a room and walked the streets for many weeks looking for work, but to no avail.

Winters out West come suddenly and quite early in the season. It was the beginning of October and raining every day. Gradually it turned to freezing rain. Edmonton was dismal. Dark gray clouds hung low over the city and a north-east wind blew the lifeless leaves in all directions.

Bernie was lying on his bed unable to sleep. He constantly worried about the unpredictable tomorrow and the days that would follow. That evening rain drenched the discoloured house, and the small window pane became encrusted with ice. He put on his coat and walked out into the frigid wind. After wandering around for several blocks, he leaned against a fence and stared into the darkness. Wrinkled yellow leaves were slowly falling from the trees, gliding gracefully through the air back and forth before landing on the wet freezing ground. In the distance a dog barked, car horns blared and now and then a light would split the darkness for a few seconds and quickly vanish.

Bernie looked at the desolate street, realizing that the rain had turned to snow. He turned around and started trudging in the direction he had come from. He felt the cold biting his face and numbing his feet. Bracing himself against gusts of wind, he trudged on, returned to his room and turned on the single light suspended on a black electric cord from the ceiling. Shingles on the roof were rattling, the wind in the chimney was whistling, and the small bulb reflecting yellowish images on the ice-covered window pane was swaying in the draught created by a strong wind outside.

Totally exhausted as if he had been walking for hours, he stretched his hands out like a child wanting to embrace the moon and whispered, "I wish I could fall asleep and have a few hours respite from the worry that's numbing my brain." He pulled out of his pocket a wrinkled sheet of paper he had once picked up in a printing shop where he was applying for a job and began reading. It was titled, "Don't Quit", and the author was not named:

> *When things go wrong, as they sometimes will,*
> *When your funds are low and your debts are high,*
> *When you want to smile, but you have to sigh,*
> *When care is pressing you down a bit —*
> *Rest if you must, but don't you quit.*
> *Life is queer with its twists and turns,*
> *As everyone of us sometimes learns,*
> *And many a fellow turns about,*
> *When he might have won had he stuck it out.*

Don't give up though the pace seems slow,
You might succeed with another blow.
Often the struggler has given up,
When he might have captured the victor's cup.
He learned too late when the night came down,
How close he was to the golden crown.
Success is failure turned inside out,
The silver tint of the clouds of doubt.
It may be near when it seems afar,
So stick to the fight when you're hardest hit,
It's when things seem worse that you musn't quit.

He read it over and over until he could no longer keep his eyes open, and finally fell asleep.

The following morning his landlady, Mrs. Ladovitch, told him that her brother, Mr. Pinkus, owned a secondhand store, and perhaps he could use him in the store for keeping the records needed for police inspectors who occasionally checked the books for stolen goods. She gave him directions and Bernie practically flew out of the house.

Mr. Pinkus was an elderly man. His hair was white, his round face full. He was short and stout and when he talked his voice sounded melodious, as if he was chanting a prayer. He sized up Bernie, inquired about his experience and background, and with a trace of a smile, told him to come to work the following morning.

On the way back to his room he began thinking and he remembered his father's words, "When things don't go right for you, and your life becomes difficult and unbearable, pray. Your prayers will be answered. Holy angels will intervene on your behalf and drive Satan away."

Bernie thought, "It sounds crazy, but then, who knows for sure? As far as I know it has never been proved one way or another. People like my father believed in superstition. Perhaps the answer to a prayer comes in a delayed reaction. By the time something good happens to you, you have forgotten that at some point in time you had prayed for it!"

One day a pretty girl appeared in the store. Her long brown hair was neatly combed, her face was thin and sensitive.

"You're new in this part of the country, aren't you? My name is Rachel, my father owns this store. What's your name?"

"My name is Bernie Appleman. I come from Winnipeg."

"Winnipeg!" she exclaimed. "I hear it's a big city. How come you decided to come to Edmonton?"

"Oh, I don't really know, I just wanted a change, I suppose."

Rachel was single. Her mother had died some years ago and her father was intending to remarry shortly. She shook his hand.

"It's nice having you working here. I'll be by again in a few days."

Rachel's visits to the store became more frequent and Bernie looked forward to them. He was falling in love. Soon after that first meeting, he proposed, and within a few weeks they married.

Mr. Pinkus suggested they live in the apartment above the store for the time being, rent-free of course. Their happiness, however, turned to despondence quickly. Mr. Pinkus was forced into bankruptcy because of the depression and retired. He remarried, as planned, and moved to Calgary where his wife owned property left to her by her first husband. As a result Bernie and Rachel were out on the street with nothing. In five years, Bernie had various short-term jobs, but never earned enough for a decent living.

Despite their financial situation, one day Bernie asked his wife, "Don't you think it's about time for us to start raising a family?"

Rachel turned pale and in a quavering voice replied, "I didn't want you to know this, but since you have brought up the subject, I might as well tell you. I have been to the doctor a number of times in the last couple of years and he finally told me a few weeks ago that I can never bear a child."

It was a shock to Bernie; his hopes were shattered.

"The only option we have is to adopt a child," Rachel

continued in a consoling tone. "As a matter of fact, the doctor intimated that he could arrange if for us within a few weeks!"

"This is the irony of fate," Bernie thought. "To most people having children is as natural as breathing, but we have to be the exception."

They adopted a baby boy. They named him Michael. It seemed, at the time, that they would live happily ever after, but that was not to be. One evening, while Bernie was browsing through a newspaper, an advertisement caught his attention. It read, "Seeking ambitious partner with some experience, for an established men's wear store, investment not necessary." He showed it to his wife and remarked, "It sounds interesting, doesn't it?" He searched her face, waiting for a reply.

"My dear Bernie," she finally responded, "I have a feeling that there is more to it than the ad is saying, and besides, you have worked very hard for many years. We have saved fifteen hundred dollars by denying ourselves necessities of life. What would happen if you were asked to invest that money? Wouldn't you be taking a risk? You don't even know the man!"

"I'll find out more about it tomorrow", he replied.

He was overwhelmingly impressed when he met the man who owned the store. He appeared to be a generous philanthropist, a most compassionate individual who was mainly interested in assisting Bernie by having him established as an equal partner in his lucrative business. Bernie was persuaded to invest the money he had, and hoped for the best.

The year that followed was the most frustrating in Bernie's life. The store was like a huge barn, dark, dreary and hopeless. Its condition made Bernie curse the day he embarked on this venture. With the slightest rain-fall, or melting of snow, water would drip throught the ceiling, ruining merchandise and spreading all over the floor. Such situations would usually occur on Saturdays, as if they were pre-arranged to disrupt the weekend business which Bernie badly needed. In desperation, Bernie would search the basement for containers, pails, or empty paint cans, placing them where the water was dripping, but it was impossible to cover all leaking spots. He would use a heavy duty mop, trying to keep some areas dry. By the time he arrived home it would be ten o'clock in the evening. He was tired, disgusted and of course worried, hoping that the leaking would stop by Sunday morning, when he and Rachel would go to the store to clean up.

After a year or more of unending struggle, the landlord who, ironically, was his silent partner, finally decided one day to patch up the leaky roof, and business began to show signs of improvement.

By the third year Bernie managed to install some extra lighting, had the store painted, and through relentless tireless effort and innovative window displays, the store was gradually transformed into a prosperous prestigious business. An image of confidence and credibility was slowly being established with his customers and Bernie was proud of the small measure of success he had achieved, simply because he refused to surrender to what he then thought was his darkest hour of adversity.

Bernie never gave up, even though the odds were against him from the very first day when he was conned by the unscrupulous partner into a hopeless situation. Now it seemed as though the worst of this experience was about over, and a ray of hope was starting to penetrate into their lives.

Business was good and getting better with each passing week, money was coming in by the thousands, which Bernie gladly kept handing over to his partner, who gave him a solemn promise that he would be using it to purchase income-producing properties. However, as time brought no action from his partner Bernie began demanding his share of the money back. But his partner just laughed and told Bernie that he would be destroying the empire which he had built over the years if he were to persist with his demands.

Bernie and Rachel spent sleepless nights trying to figure out a way to free themselves from the tyrant.

Some of Bernie's friends told him that he was not the first victim to suffer at the hands of this tormentor, who had done much harm to others through the years, while projecting a false image of important philanthropy in the community.

One morning when he arrived at the store, Bernie found that the door lock had been changed since he had left the place the evening before. Angrily he called his partner and demanded an explanation.

"I have purposely changed the lock to teach you a lesson" his partner said, "you're not to pester me for money."

From time to time Bernie met his partner only when a business meeting required it. They usually met at night, at the rear of the store. Bernie never forgot one particular session when he begged his partner to pay him at least some of the money owing to him. His associate just laughed.

"You're crazy", the man said. "the fifty thousand dollars you claim I owe you you'll never see. Better still — start whistling and get the hell out of here or I'll use this on your yellow belly."

With that, the partner seized a pair of scissors from the counter and aimed the glistening points at Bernie's midriff.

Fearing for his life, Bernie darted for the door.

Despite the threat, Bernie returned to the store and on the next visit of his partner broke the cold silence between them by again asking for what was due him. When that failed, Bernied modified his appeal by saying, "At least you should give me back the fifteen hundred dollars I invested when I first went into partnership with you."

"Not a dime!" the other answered. "Furthermore, if I ever see you here again, your life won't be worth a penny. This is the last time I ever want to see you."

Bernie could think of no further way to break down his partner's resistance — he had no choice but to surrender to this crazy reality. For the last time he walked, slowly and uncertainly, from the place where he and his wife had given so much of their lives and their limited means, where they had worked together so hard to build a business that had become both prestigious and lucrative, and from which the merciless partner was ejecting them.

It was four o'clock in the morning when Bernie got home.

Rachel was waiting for him. Bernie told her everything. They talked till dawn broke over the city. They went to bed, troubled as never before in their married life.

After a sleepless few hours, Bernie rose. It was mid-morning, but there was no sound or movement from Rachel. He tiptoed from the room and had his breakfast. By this time Bernie was feeling somewhat uneasy. It was not like Rachel to sleep so late. He returned to the bedroom.

"Rachel, Rachel — it's time to get up," he said. But there was no response. Bernie moved to the side of the bed and looked down at his wife. She did not move even when he touched her. Her eyes were open, but, if they saw anything, there was no physical response.

The doctor who came in answer to Bernie's frantic telephone call had little difficulty in the diagnosis — Rachel had suffered a paralyzing stroke. She was alive, but that was about all.

Rachel's illness was a devastating blow to Bernie. There was only one compensation in his tortured life, and that was the support given to him by their son Michael, a gifted musician, a genius. At the age of ten he was performing on his violin some of the most difficult concertos with leading symphony orchestras and was taking part in solo recitals. He won many awards and music critics across Canada had nothing but praise for his performances. They were sure that he had a brilliant future on the concert stages of the world.

Unfortunately, Bernie's financial loss, and Rachel's stroke, affected Michael deeply. It was obvious that he was gradually losing his enthusiasm for performing. Nevertheless he kept on taking part in music competitions across Canada, winning most of them.

Bernie tried to make a new start. He sold everything he could lay his hands on. He made a low down payment on a fifty-acre farm a few miles out of town and moved his sick wife and son Michael into a small two-room shack. Neighbourhood farmers came to his assistance and he, in turn, repaid them by helping them plant the seed or harvest the crops, and saved a dollar whenever possible to pay for Michael's music lessons.

Miracles, however, do happen. One day during that trying period an exploration company, searching for oil in the area, approached Bernie and asked for permission to drill on his farm. A few months later derricks could be seen everywhere on the once parched unproductive prairie, and the poor insignificant farmers were becoming rich from the royalties they were collecting and Bernie had three oil rigs on his own farm. It was a captivating sight to see oil - black gold - being pumped out of the ground.

Within a few years Bernie acquired a fortune. He had a new luxurious home, a guest house, and a swimming pool built on his property. His wife, though, remained vegetating in bed. For the time being, money couldn't save her. Over the years of Rachel's illness, Michael had become melancholy and deeply depressed. He no longer concentrated on the music that was so dear to him, and he refused to enter the competitions in which he excelled. Then came the day that Michael failed to join Bernie at breakfast and did not respond to repeated calls at his closed bedroom door. Bernie at last opened the door and was struck with horror to find Michael dead in his bed. Michael, the family physician later told Bernie, had died by his own hand, from an overdose of sleeping pills. There was little doubt, the doctor said, that the illness of his beloved mother had grown from worry to complete despondency and finally driven him to end his own life.

Rachel made helpless by the stroke, and her speech impaired, was aware of the tragedy, Bernie realized. Her lamentations made it even more difficult for Bernie to live with this second tribulation. As she wailed again and again, he managed to make out words among the jumble of sounds pouring from her mouth. Bernie finally made sense out of them.

"How could Michael have done this to us? It's wrong for parents to outlive their children — it's a sin against nature," she lamented.

Within a few days Rachel sank into a coma, withdrawing into her own silent world, oblivious to her surroundings.

Bernie never shed a tear. He sat in the living room, his eyes glued to the ceiling, his senses paralyzed by the sudden shock. He was unable to fathom the depth of the tragedy, his whole life shattered. For days messages of condolence poured in, the telephone kept on ringing, friends enquired about his and Rachel's condition. Then the calls and visits dwindled to nothing. That upset Bernie, who told his closest neighbour:

"I hate seeing the way most of my friends and acquaintances look at me as though suicide was a shameful act and I'm the guilty one. People are whispering about me, some of them evade me as if I had committed a crime. I hate going out because of the way they're avoiding me, they have nothing to say to me. I get the silent treatment."

This was too much for one of Bernie's best friends to take, he invited Bernie home. When he got there, Bernie broke down and sobbed uncontrollably. As soon as the crying subsided, his friend spoke directly and firmly, "You're an intelligent man, Bernie. You know that what has happened cannot be changed — it's irreversible. Your behaviour, the way you mistakenly think that people blame you for what has occurred — that's all wrong. What you are saying about good friends and neighbours is all a mistake and won't alter the situation. You still have Rachel to care for, and you can help her best by accepting the respect and goodwill of your friends and by not believing you are being accused of any wrongdoing."

Bernie said nothing.

At home, Bernie gave almost constant attention to Rachel's welfare, but there was little he could do. On medical advice, Bernie had her admitted to a hospital. Two months later the doctor said that nothing more could be done for her there, at which time Bernie thought that she would be better off at home.

In time, Bernie regained and resumed his active life, as though with every personal tragedy his inner strength had increased, helping him to cope with the impossible. His determination could perhaps have been in part attributed to his Chassidic upbringing. Although he had severed all ties with religion many years before and he no longer prayed as he once did, the values his parents had taught him helped him to survive in the face of disastrous calamities.

God, Bernie felt, had been good to him, especially in blessing him with the wisdom to buy the farm on which oil had been found, a discovery that had enriched him far beyond any of his youthful dreams. On the other hand, if there was a reward, there was also punishment. But why was he being punished so severely, why had God inflicted such tragedies upon him? He thought about god a good deal; indeed, he often began his thoughts about the Deity with the words, "Dear God".

Why did he say, "Dear God", Bernie asked himself. Was it habit? He did not really know what had happened between him and God. He remembered the traditions and the teachings of his parents and he never forgot that he was the grandson of a Chassidic rabbi. When he thought about prayer, he recalled what the Danish author Isak Dinesen had written, that "prayer is the service of the heart. People pray because they can't help praying." At one time Bernie had had something tangible and valuable — a silent communication between him and God — but that had been lost in his years of sorrow, little by little eaten away, eroded by disappointment, adversity, and grief.

Bernie remained on the farm, with a housekeeper, who doubled as a nurse for Rachel, and a farmhand to attend to the day-to-day chores. Bernie sat for hours each day at his wife's bedside. As the events of the stormy past moved through his head, he often wondered, "What gives memories their power to evoke emotion? Perhaps it's their completeness, because complete joy leaves us strengthened, and fails to give us a reason for suffering. But anything that's worth suffering for is worth loving." He had become resigned to his destiny in life, and memories, happy and sad, were now an integral part of his existence.

One problem with life on the farm was isolation — almost all of his friends lived in Edmonton and rarely visited him except by invitation. Seldom did he drop in on the closest neighbour and good friend who had talked to him so frankly at the time of the death of Michael. They had drifted apart for no particular reason;

when they did meet, on some special occasion, they greeted each other with words of rejoicing, they promised that they must see each other more often but they never did.

Then Bernie's dull, monotonous life took on a new dimension as a result of the exciting meeting with his childhood friends in Winnipeg. It would be wonderful if they could all get together again, this time in the peace and quiet of the Appleman farm, Bernie decided. He immediately invited all of those he had met by such remarkable chance. As he awaited their replies, he could hardly contain the excitement.

CHAPTER 17

To Bernie's friends and guests, it seemed as if the whole world was unwinding and relaxing in the summer sunshine.

In the fenced-in yard, a dog barked, a cow scratched herself against a post, roosters crowed and two horses dozed in a corner of the wooden fence, eyes half closed as though they were meditating, resting their heads on each other's necks. Occasionally they glanced sideways, flicking their tales to shake off the mosquitoes. When a rabbit scurried from bush to bush, the horses perked up their ears momentarily, then returned to their somnolent position.

Bernie and his friends were sitting on the guest house balcony, mesmerized by the brightness of the full moon and the starry sky. They could almost hear angels singing. Brigette broke the silence:

"I am simply intoxicated by all this. After so many years in a city, it's beyond comprehension how bewitching a clear summer night on a farm can really be."

Ingi got up, stretched, and said, "How about driving into town and seeing a movie? What do you say, guys?"

Andy was interested. Bernie, to be polite, also agreed.

"I am very tired and couldn't possibly sit through a movie, Ruben said. "I would only be spoiling your fun."

"I think I'll pass and take a rain cheque," said Brigette. "You fellows go ahead. I think I'll turn in. It's been a long day."

The men left Ruben and Brigette on the balcony. It was fascinating for them to lie on the lounge and look up at the stars through the tree branches. Pierre suddenly appeared.

"Can I be of some service to you before I retire for the night?" he asked.

"Yes," Ruben said, "There is cold beer in the refrigerator. Pour a couple of glasses, please."

Pierre promptly served the beer, then discreetly retired.

Ruben and Brigette went indoors with their drinks. In the living room, Ruben leafed through a book. Brigette watched him secretly with her green eyes that appeared greener than usual in the bright lights. She noticed his hands trembling. She walked over to the sofa, sat down beside him and asked, "Are you upset?"

"Not really," he replied, "I'm just feeling somewhat anxious for no reason other than the usual self-recrimination."

"About what?" she persisted.

"I have become obsessed with a feeling that, had I noticed Helga's symptoms sooner, she might be alive today!"

"Ruben, for an intelligent business man, you talk like a fool! There comes a time in everyone's life when we helplessly stand by, seeing things clearly leading to something traumatic, but are unable to stop, or even impede their progress."

He suddenly turned to her and whispered, "Thank you for staying with me, your presence is very important to me."

Arm in arm they went back to the balcony gazing at the sky full of stars. Small ones, large ones, in clusters scattered in all directions. "Brigette, reach out with your hand and catch a star!" Ruben said.

Ruben walked into his bedroom, stretched out on the bed. "Am I tired!" he said. Brigette sat down beside him. She gently turned his face towards her, bent over and planted a passionate kiss on his lips. The windows were open and the fragrance of roses filled the room.

"You look awfully tired, let me help you undress," she said. "You'll feel better when you get under a cool bed sheet."

"You're my angel of mercy," he whispered, kissing and caressing her face. "Thank you for allowing me to hold you close to me, don't deny me a bit of heaven," he pleaded.

She slid into bed beside him, her beautiful long hair covering the pillow. He buried his face in her bosom. "How wonderful life can sometimes be!" he whispered. "A moment like this makes up for all the yesterdays. I'm really not asking you for anything more, I might not be able to reciprocate," he said quietly.

After a while, however, powers long dormant began stirring within him. He kissed her again and again, he spoke of other romances that passed quickly and were forgotten, with one exception: Helga. He knew he would cherish her memory forever. Sparks of passion, however, ignited into a flame. Not even in his youth had he known such overwhelming desire. He threw off his blanket and gazed longingly at Brigette. She was breathing heavily in anticipation. He saw Helga's face for a split second just before complete passion engulfed them.

Brigette had waited for just such an opportunity. He pressed her closer to his body and could hear drums beating in his ears. The room was spinning, whirling into infinity. The moon and the stars suddenly united into one ball of fire, the ball exploded, leaving tiny fragments suspended in mid-air, hot sparks gradually disintegrated and dissolved into the night.

Ruben woke up a few hours later, got out of bed and stood nude at the open window. The prairies were still asleep, resting on the wings of night. He looked at the bed and noticed that Brigette was sound asleep. "I have never believed in miracles, but one just happened. Special moments that make memories are very seldom planned," he thought.

A cool breeze was softly caressing him, cooling his perspiring body. He closed his eyes and opened his mouth wide, inhaling the deep, crisp, refreshing air. He glanced at Brigette again and thought, "She certainly made me feel like a man again, even though I didn't think it was possible." He rubbed his hands together thinking, "Best get best, winners stay winners. Next to Helga, Brigette is most desirable and enjoyable to be with." Ruben quietly edged his way back into bed and fell asleep.

It is morning on the farm. The sun is rising from the depths of the flat prairie. Here and there a bird flies by. Roosters are crowing and flapping their wings. A cat is gingerly walking on grass, carefully trying not to wet its paws in the pearly dew. Ruben and Brigette are sitting at the pool-side, thinking about the gratifying night they had together.

"Have you ever loved anyone for real?" Brigette asked.

"At some point in my life I thought I had. I have always been very discreet about it though. You see, Brigette," Ruben confessed, "ever since I can remember, I have never tasted the meaning or the feeling of being loved by anyone. Consequently, I grew up unloved, and had no love to share with others. There were some short periods of time in my life when I was quite fond of someone, but I couldn't take the risk of showing it openly, always expecting to be rejected if I did. My first encounter which I thought was true love was Laura. She took me in, gave me food, a place to sleep and, of course, her love. For the first time in my live I loved and I was being loved in return.

"As I got to understand it later, I realized that it was no more than gratitude on my part. Later, when, just by chance, I met Helga, I pretended that I loved her, because of pure selfish motivation. I had a feeling of loving her because of anticipated success. With the passing of time, however, I realized that I really and truly loved her, not only for material gains, but for what she represented. She was everything any man could wish for; even if she had been poor, I would have loved her."

"Do you love me?" Brigette phrased her question carefully.

"My dear," he replied, "love based on sex alone is not true love. At my age I have other ways of expressing that feeling. Sure, I have feelings for you, but not as a young romantic. Their expectations in life are in a way unrealistic, and yet they dream beautiful dreams about passion and romance. They are infatuated with each other's foolish dreams and desires, which seldom materialize. I admire you, I respect you, and I think that you deserve a lot more from life than what you are getting. I promise you, though, that as long as I'm well, I shall see that no harm comes to you. I'll watch over you and enjoy your presence!"

"Thank you, Ruben, for being honest. I appreciate it, coming from you it's quite a compliment!"

She slipped away to her own room as the lights of Bernie's car flickered in the windows.

Sunday was a dull dreary day on the farm. Dark clouds hung low and there was a light rain. The yard, where chickens or a cow would normally be seen, was deserted. The friends gathered in Bernie's main house and talked about many things, including the farm and the tragedies they endured through the years. Rachel, assisted by her nurse, sat motionless, slouched in her wheel chair, her watery eyes looking into space. It was depressing, yet no one dared to change the subject.

Ingi reached for Brigette's hand and their eyes met. "Let's go back to the guest house," he whispered.

When they stood up to go, Andy jokingly suggested, "How about catching some gophers tomorrow — you have gophers here haven't you?"

Bernie smiled crookedly and replied, "We had a great time doing it, didn't we? Unfortunately, such an exciting experience is only for the young!"

The magic spell that the farm had cast over the visitors on their arrival had been broken by the inexplicable depression that fell over the group. There was only one thing to do — they said their appreciative farewells and by the middle of the week were on their way back to Winnipeg.

CHAPTER 18

Dawn was breaking when Ruben got out of bed. He parted the window drapes and yawned. "It was a wonderful vacation," he thought. "I find it hard to forget Bernie and his poor wife. She must have been a beautiful woman before she was stricken by that horrible illness." He continued to think about the years that flew by so quickly and about the miraculous meeting of his friends. He realized that he had a lot to be thankful for. He was thinking about some men his age he had met since he returned and, surprisingly, no one talked about old age or admitted being dejected because of it. There were some odd complaints, ranging from sexual impotence to minor depression, because body functions no longer responded as quickly or efficiently as in the past. Otherwise, no one appeared to have any serious problems.

Andy came in and joined Ruben at the window. "It looks like it's going to be a nice day after the haze lifts," he said.

"Yes," Ruben replied dryly.

"Ingi is off today, I'm going to ask him to spend a few hours with me in Kildonan Park, perhaps Brigette would also join us. Would you care to come too?

"Why not?" Ruben replied.

After breakfast, Ruben knocked on Pierre's door but there was no response. He cautiously entered the room and found the bed neat and tidy. It appeared that it had not been touched during the night. He searched the entire penthouse and the underground parking area. The limousine was covered with dust from the trip, but Pierre was nowhere to be found. Several hours later he appeared. He looked tired, dishevelled, and out of sorts. He proceeded to apologize to Ruben for his behaviour.

"I know you are disappointed, and I don't blame you, but

things somehow happen. We change and blindly follow our instinct, only to be sorry later. I'm sorry if I caused you needless worry and anxiety by my absence."

"Pierre", Ruben interjected, "you have been a loyal friend for many years, punctual and honest. What happened that brought about this sudden change in you?"

"Brigette called me yesterday and told me that Ingi was leaving town for a few days. Would I be so kind as to keep her company for a little while."

"Why didn't you tell me about it?" Ruben fumed.

"I didn't think you would miss me for a few hours."

"You call a whole night a few hours? Remember, loyalty is the highest form of morality, which I never questioned as far as you were concerned!"

Pierre continued to recount how Brigette manipulated him to this embarrassing situation. "She was daring me, tempting me, saying among other things, 'Don't you crave a woman, what do you have in your veins, blood or sour milk?'

"I begged her not to tease me and told her I had to return, but she persisted, until I gave in to her demands.

"You are a man," he said to Ruben, "you ought to know the feeling!"

"I know, I know," he said. I understand. But you should have told me you were going out."

Pierre was nervous. He had never succumbed to temptation before, but last night was different. He turned, facing Ruben and said, "I regret the incident, sir, but I was unable to leave sooner."

"Did you sleep with her?"

"Mr. Ruben, calm yourself down, we are all human, there comes a time in everyone's life when temptation overpowers the mind. In all the years I have been with you I never once indulged in this sort of relationship. Last night, however, I found it irresistible. She sort of lured me in until there was no escape!"

Over the next few days, the friendship and loyalty between employer and chauffeur deteriorated. There was less and less communication between them. Finally, Pierre gathered up his courage, walked into the living room, and confronted Ruben.

"Sir, may I have a word with you?"

"Yes, of course, what about?"

"Well sir," Pierre hesitantly began, "I have given a lot of thought to what I am about to say, and have come to the conclusion that I must try to bring about some sort of change to my life. We are all getting on in years and time waits for no one. I have served you loyally for many years, never thinking about my own personal needs. Lately, however, I began worrying about my future, what's left of it, and of course my advanced age. As you know, sir, I have been a loner most of my life, and never thought I would be needing someone to share my final few years, but my thinking has changed. By coincidence I met a lady who is seeking my companionship and for the first time in my life, I realize that I could be quite happy in sharing my remaining years with her. She owns a small cottage in St. Boniface and is waiting for the day for me to propose to her."

Ruben was surprised, "Why would you even entertain the idea of getting married at your age? Is it sex you are looking for? If it is, Brigette could very well look after that."

"I haven't had any sex in over twenty years until the other night, and I could easily do without it! It's companionship that I need. Now is my chance to think realistically and I have come to a definite decision. I will, however, stay on if you'll have me, until you get someone suitable to replace me."

Ruben thanked Pierre and shook his hand, saying, "You were my closest and most loyal friend when I needed you. I won't ever forget that! If this is your wish, good luck to you. He moved towards the door, then turned, sat down at his desk, wrote a cheque and handed it to Pierre. "Here, take this with my blessing!"

Pierre, with tears in his eyes, replied, "Thank you sir, I'll forever be grateful to you for your generosity and understanding." He turned and walked out of the room, just as Andy entered.

"What's the matter with him?" Andy asked. Ruben told him.

"Brigette is really making the rounds." Andy said. "Even poor Pierre didn't manage to escape her."

"She must be most unhappy with Ingi," Ruben calmly replied. He felt his heart miss a beat and continued, "I'm convinced that Ingi has been indulging in sex with other women lately, and I am sure Brigette knows about it. She is confused, unhappy and is therefore reacting by having an occasional affair with men she knows."

"What makes you think so?" Andy queried.

"I have heard stories about Ingi from reliable sources," Ruben remarked with certainty.

"I would be inclined to disagree with you," Andy countered. "I think that she is a promiscuous woman who hangs herself on any 'Joe Blow' she meets."

"I'm not about to agree with your opinion, you are judging her too harshly. She is a female, sharing her femininity only within the circle of her friends!" Ruben asserted, then abruptly changed the subject.

"Andy, are you a good driver?" he suddenly inquired.

"Why do you ask?"

"When Pierre leaves, I would like you to drive my limousine. I am at the moment not interest in hiring a replacement."

"I think I could handle it," Andy agreed. "I remember driving a huge soft drink truck the first few years we lived in Montreal."

"Would you want me to order a chauffeur's uniform for you with the name 'Pierre' on it?"

"Don't be smart with me, my friend, or I'll refuse to warm up your milk before bedtime!" They shook hands and had a hearty laugh.

Labour Day weather in Winnipeg can be unpredictable. Ruben and Andy drove out together on a balmy Labour Day. When they reached Portage and Main, they realized they had forgotten about the customary holiday parade. The sidewalks were jammed with spectators waiting for the marching bands and the ear-piercing wail of bagpipes, the thundering drums, and the catcalls directed at the husky men in kilts. They parked on a side street while Ruben and Andy watched the parade, until Ruben, announcing that the noise had given him a headache, decided to go home.

No sooner had they arrived at the apartment than Brigette burst in. Her hair was a mess, her face smudged, and her eyes red from crying.

"I need your help — please, please, help me!" she cried in a trembling voice.

Ruben and Andy tried to calm her down.

"I've been living through hell with Ingi" she said, "I suspected he was having sex with other women. I've seen him meeting women on the street corners and men too! He'd disappear with them for hours. He now ignores me, avoids me, even though, in the kindest way, I've been trying to get him to tell me what's bothering him and why he's become oblivious to my very existence.

"This morning I went to work, even though it is a holiday. Ingi knew I was going, but he didn't say anything. A couple of hours later I felt ill and decided I'd go home. Ingi was in bed with a young woman, while another one stood there — waiting her turn. I screamed and ran for the door. Ingi ran after me, caught up with me on the street, and threatened me.

'You say one word to anyone about what you have just seen, your life won't be worth a dime!' Then he walked away. What am I to do now, how can I possibly bear the humiliation?" She folded up like a deflated doll, sat down on the floor and cried bitterly. Ruben sat down beside her.

"You have known about his past, you were also aware that he sometimes had sex with other women," Ruben said. "It shouldn't be such a shock to you."

"There is a difference in knowing something but not really believing it, and seeing with your own eyes," she lamented.

Andy remained silent.

Ruben suggested to Brigette that she live in his penthouse until things settled down a bit and tempers cooled off. She accepted on the condition that she would do the cooking and look after the

146

apartment. This Ruben emphatically rejected.

"I have a maid who does the cooking and the cleaning. You are my guest and will be treated as such! Please don't worry," he said. "I don't intend to send you away into the desert with nothing but a jug of water, as Abraham did to Hagar!"

Weeks passed. Winnipeg was in the grip of freezing temperatures and heavy snow. Some days the streets were almost impassable, and the nights bitterly cold. It happened on such an evening. The three friends were whiling the time away in warm comfort, when the ringing of the telephone broke through the tranquil silence. Ruben picked up the phone and listened to a man's voice. It sounded incoherent and yet he thought he detected something familiar in it.

"Who is this?" he finally asked.

"It's me, Ingi!"

"Where are you?"

"I have been out for days and nights searching for Brigette!" he lamented, "I'm now in a phone booth a few blocks away. Have you seen or heard from her in the last few days?" Ruben hesitated, then replied, "As a matter of fact, she is here right now!"

"Can I come up to see her?" Ingi asked.

"Not after what you have done to her," Ruben sharply replied.

"Ruben, you are my friend, help me, you know how much Brigette and I love each other. I can't live without her!"

"You should have thought of that before. I have a feeling that you'll survive with your other friends! Brigette, Andy and I refuse to see you again, or be your friends, after your shameful act in front of Brigette. She has had enough of you, the sooner you get that through your head, the better!"

"You mean you're refusing to let me see her?"

"You've got it. If I were you, I'd leave town!"

"Ruben, please," Ingi pleaded.

Brigette couldn't resist the temptation of saying something. She took the phone out of Ruben's hand and in a controlled voice said, "Ingi, through the years we loved each other dearly, you were my king, and I was proud of being your queen; unfortunately, one never knows how much loving someone is going to cost until one starts paying for it. We had our disagreements, but we were mature enough that we always found a way to compromise. Time will never bring us together again, nor will it heal the wounds you inflicted upon me. Don't ever call me again!"

With a trembling hand she hung up the phone, wiping large tears off her face. "It was too good to last," she whispered.

A few days later Ruben was alone in his suite, in deep contemplation. The constant ringing of his telephone, though, interferred with his concentration. He picked up the receiver and in an irritable voice shouted, "Who is it, and what do you want?"

He was surprised to hear Ingi say, "Hello friend, I am sorry to disappoint you by having to inform you that I am still in town. I didn't disappear as you and Brigette had hoped I would. I thought that I should first remind you of our gratifying relationship in Stockholm. You were lonely, broken-hearted, and willingly accepted me as your friend. We had some great times together, didn't we?"

"Come to the point," Ruben curtly interjected.

"If you want me to leave town or the country, it's going to cost you," Ingi laughingly replied.

Ruben, biting his lips to control his anger, demanded, "What makes you think that I would pay you in order to have you leave the country?"

"Because I know too much about your past and your sexual activities which you so eagerly shared with me. I could spread this information among your rich friends, and that could harm your prestige and your reputation."

Ruben was almost burning up with fury, but controlled his voice. "This is blackmail," he said calmly.

"Call it what you wish. I want twenty thousand dollars for disappearing out of your life forever," Ingi quietly replied. "That's not too high a price for a wealthy man like you, is it?"

"How do I know that you'll keep your promise?" Ruben

asked, somewhat disarmed.

"You don't. You'll have to trust me. You have no choice", Ingi replied. 'I'll be waiting for you in the Holiday Inn lobby tomorrow morning at ten o'clock, and you better be there. So long, sucker!" and he hung up.

The following morning Ruben was at the hotel by ten and found Ingi sitting in a deep chair leafing through a magazine. He dropped a cheque in Ingi's lap, and said, "Here is your blackmail money and I hope you choke spending it". Ingi examined the cheque and was satisfied to see that it was certified. He focused his eyes on Ruben and said in a consoling voice: "You ought to know that we gays are honourable people, and always keep our promise. I assure you that you and Brigette will never see nor hear from me again".

He offered his hand in a gesture of friendship. "You are despicable and disgusting!" Ruben said and stormed out of the hotel.

Winter was over. Balmy southern breezes drifted across the tranquil sky. Ruben sat beside Brigette on a bench in the park and meditated on life. "How beautiful and serene life could have been if I only had taken the time to observe nature and enjoy it," he thought. "Instead, I devoted most of my life to making money. Thanks to Helga, I succeeded. Brigette perhaps could make my life a bit more pleasant, if I could only learn to love her the way I would want to, which seems impossible at the present time. I pity her, I tolerate her, but I can't truly love her, not just yet. No one can fill the void in my heart which was once occupied by someone special, even though I often think that perhaps she could infuse me with a new interest and a more positive approach in dealing with life.

I have always believed that creativity and anticipation keep one young and alert. I have been struggling for several years now without Helga, trying, but not succeeding, to be reborn.

"The most difficult thing in the world is to smile when your heart is breaking. Loneliness revealed to me that beyond the first pangs of desolation, terror, anguish and grief, I had to find a key to

149

a deeper insight of myself, if I was to survive.

"I found my friends and got to know Brigette, who perhaps would be capable of turning me around and showing me some daylight, make me forget the thousands of yesterdays when every day was New Year's, every woman was a Queen and I was a King, and the sun was shining even on rainy days."

He shook Brigette gently. "The sun is rising, it's time to get up!"

She sat up, looking a bit bewildered. "Why did you let me fall asleep?" she asked.

"That's O.K., I did some hard thinking in the meantime," he replied.

"What about?" she wanted to know.

"About us and Ingi."

"I still can't believe that he has gone out of my life!"

"Believe it!" Ruben assured her.

"What if he were to show up again, what would I do? We don't even know where he is or what he is intending to do", Brigette asked.

"We haven't heard from him since the day you came over crying. I have a feeling that he might have left town, or perhaps the country," Ruben replied. He had concealed from Brigette the fact of Ingi's blackmail and intended not to tell her of it.

"I hope you're right," Brigette whispered, almost prayerfully as she linked her arm in his and walked home.

Ruben made a few inquiries the following day and was informed by some of Ingi's friends that he had indeed left the country, and was now back in Sweden. Brigette raised her hands to the heavens and exclaimed, "Thank God! I only hope he never returns!"

A few days later they strolled in the park again and Ruben finally offered her a well conceived proposition.

"You see, Brigette," Ruben hesitatingly began, "it would be unfair on my part if I were to tell you that I'm deeply in love with you. I am very fond of you, though, in spite of your recent strange behaviour. Given some time, however, I believe that we would learn to love one another. We need each other and would most likely enjoy a happy normal relationship. But, on my conditions!"

"May I know what they are?" Brigette inquired.

Ruben, in a serious tone, continued, "I don't believe that two mature adults like us should be contemplating a traditional marriage — sign your name on a piece of paper, and get a license the way you would legalize owning a pet. My feeling is that we could live just as happily, with respect, dignity and affection for each other, without a license."

He cupped her face with both hands, looked into her green eyes and asked, "What do you say?"

"I am perfectly willing if you are," she replied. They embraced and sealed their promise with a long passionate kiss.

"I have substantial incomes from Switzerland and Spain to provide for you the best kind of life money can buy," Ruben told her.

"I hope you are not doing this out of pity?" she cautiously remarked.

"Let me just say that I am feeling sorry for both of us and I think that we both have a great deal to gain by this arrangement," he replied.

"Thank you," she managed to say, then began to sob.

"Why are you crying?" he asked.

"Because you have just made me the happiest woman in the world. Women cry when they are happy and also when they are miserable. Happy crying, however, makes one feel good."

"Are you feeling better now?" he asked.

"Much, much better," she reassured him, as she dried her eyes.

Arm in arm they walked out of the park. Ruben hailed a cab and they got lost in the rush-hour traffic. He leaned back and thought, "Well, I never believed that I could possibly do this noble act. I'm proud of myself!"

To celebrate the occasion they bought flowers, wine, cognac and cakes on the way home. The flowers were placed on the table which they covered with a white linen table cloth, and they waited nervously for Andy to come in, to surprise him with the exciting news.

Daylight had surrendered to the dark of night, but they remained sitting in the dark living room, waiting for the moment when Andy would appear in the doorway. Suddenly the full blast of blazing lights came on, turning the penthouse into a glittering castle.

"Surprise, surprise," Brigette and Ruben shouted in unison. "Andy, congratulate us, we are almost married!"

Andy froze in his tracks, his mouth open. "What do you mean, almost married?" he asked.

"We are going to live together!" Ruben explained.

"I wish you both many years of love, health and happiness. I'm very happy for you both!" Andy assured them.

His good wishes, however, sounded flat and empty; he didn't quite succeed in expressing his enthusiasm as would be expected on such an occasion. There was an obvious lack of sincerity in his wishes. From the expression on Andy's face and the nervous twitching of his right eye, it was clear that he had mixed feelings about the unexpected news and wished he could express them to Ruben. However, he remained silent and went to his room.

"How odd is the irony of fate," he thought. "I never would have dreamed that in spite of everything that's happened in the last few months, Ruben would accept Brigette on such simple, unorthodox terms. I don't blame him. In a way it's selfless, there comes a time in everyone's life when thought must change to action, and Ruben is no exception."

With Ingi in Sweden, Bernie in Edmonton, Ruben and Brigette in the equivalent of marriage, what now was in store for him — what did he have to look forward to? Andy pondered his future for many hours — what should he do?

CHAPTER 19

Andy, seated on the balcony of Ruben's penthouse, watched a blackbird perched on the railing. The bird reminded him of the vast reaches of the prairies where he had lived as a child. He recalled how the flocks of birds would careen overhead in the fresh early morning sunshine. Over everything there was the blue sky, with puffs of cottony clouds floating like white pillows that gradually dissolved against the horizon. On such mornings God's light fell on everything, on the bushes, on the grass, on the flowers. The cows were grazing contentedly in the pasture, the horses stood neck to neck by the fence, mutely exchanging information.

The beauty of the early morning that was dawning on this particular day reminded Andy of his yesterdays, yet he could not shake from his mind the uncertainty of his tomorrows. He looked down from the balcony to the still sleeping city below. The streets were deserted. The only sounds disturbing the quiet of dawn were the faint puffing of trains, clanking of wheels and an occasional screech of brakes from the distant railway yards. All was right with the world — but not for Andy.

The events of recent days were uppermost in his mind, especially when he considered what he should or could do. "Ruben has Brigette, Bernie has gone back West, even Pierre has someone. My circle is shrinking and, if I'm to have any happiness in life, I have to do something about it. Perhaps I should look harder for Esther — she is my only hope, if I can find her. But I *must* find her!"

"Good morning, Andy," Ruben said. "It's a glorious day, isn't it?" was his greeting as he looked at the beauty below.

"I guess so", replied Andy, glumly.

"Why the doom and gloom on such a beautiful day?"

"I've been thinking."

"About what?"

"About Esther. She's always in my mind, as you know. And I've told you how I've looked for her back East, in Montreal and in Toronto. I've looked everywhere in Winnipeg, but never found a trace of her. Now I'm thinking that maybe she went farther west, probably to one of the bigger cities, because she had spent most of her life in big places like Winnipeg and Montreal. If she was trying to avoid meeting people who would know her, she might well have gone to a city like Calgary or Edmonton, or even Vancouver. What do you think, Ruben?"

"It's possible", Ruben conceded. This confirmation of his idea made Andy more certain that his intuition was right. He pressed on:

"Ruben, would you be willing to drive me out West for a visit with Bernie? He's insisted, again and again, that he wants us to come out for another stay with him. If we took him up on that, I could use his place as a base for a look around Edmonton."

"I'll be glad to go, as long as you do the driving", Ruben said.

A few days later they were on their way. The last few miles of the long journey were in fog that shrouded the countryside. The side road which led to Bernie's farm was almost impassable. The car windows fogged up and the limousine kept fishtailing as they got on to a short muddy road leading to Bernie's house. The deep ditches on either side were brimming with murky water. In the fields, brown stubble and grass looked distinctly yellow against the dark puddled earth. Oil derricks scattered in the area appeared like ghosts, almost invisible through the rain and haze that enveloped everything.

A farm on rainy days isn't the most pleasant place to be, especially for city folks. You have to be a seasoned farmer to cope. Bernie made them all comfortable in the guest house and lit a fire. They were content to sit and listen to the logs crackling, slowly burning, in an atmosphere of tranquility. It rained for several days during which they made plans.

"Bernie," Andy suggested one day, "we are strangers in this part of the country, whereas you are probably familiar with every street. Would you join Ruben and me for a few hours tomorrow?"

Although Bernie thought it was a waste of time, he nevertheless consented to the suggestion. "After all, it's my sister we are searching for, and she means more to me than anything in this world. I remember my father saying on many occasions. 'Seek and you shall find.' It's perhaps improbable but not impossible, that is, if she is alive. Miracles do happen, who knows? If that's your intuition, let's put it to a test."

In an old residential part of Edmonton, every block or two was anchored by a small corner family grocery store, which was usually minded by the wife, while the husband was working elsewhere. Most of the women who tended the stores were personal friends of their customers. This area was where the three had decided to roam and ask questions. But no one had heard of the Esther they were looking for neither by name nor by description.

Near the end of one hot and tiring day, Bernie suggested to his friends, who were exhausted and ready to call it quits, that they check one more neighbourhood. At one time the streets there had been familiar to him, especially those in the block where he had lived, long ago when he first came to Edmonton. Through the years some of the buildings had changed, others had survived the sophisticated bulldozers that had flattened many areas. Bernie remembered one house in which the living room had been converted into a store — his onetime landlady, Mrs. Latovich, had bought her groceries there. The house was still there, untouched by progress.

In the store they were met by an elderly woman, short, stout, with dishevelled gray hair. She was leaning against the counter, wheezing heavily. Ruben whispered to Andy, "I think she's Ukrainian. See if you can remember enough to talk to her in her own language." Andy nodded his agreement. He questioned the woman about her customers, their names, how long they had lived

155

in the area, and other things that might give them a clue. Years before, the woman said, the neighbourhood had been predominantly Jewish. Then, gradually, many of the Jewish people had moved to the suburbs, and their places had been taken by Ukrainians, Poles, and immigrants from other European countries.

"I know a Jewish lady," she continued, "a friend of mine who is living in one of the new suburbs. She knows most of the people that have lived around here for many years, before they gradually moved away. I don't know her last name, her first name is Sarah. She might be able to give you more information, here is her address".

They thanked her, but decided they had had enough for that day. On their way back to the car, they walked past a house that Bernie couldn't help pointing out to his friends.

"Look," he said, "this is where I lived when I first arrived here."

They stopped, and through an opening in the window drape they thought they saw a woman inside. Andy, out of curiosity, climbed a couple of steps, knocked on the door and waited.

A weak and trembling woman's voice, hardly audible, asked, "Who is it?"

"You probably don't know me, I'm a stranger in the city, but would like to have a word with you," Andy replied.

She didn't respond. Instead he heard the door latch on the inside slowly slide open. The door came ajar a bit but not enough for him to clearly see the person inside. She pressed her face into the open space and Andy fell to the verandah floor. The door quickly closed tight and the inside bolt locked. Bernie and Ruben rushed to Andy's aid, trying to revive him but failed. He was out, cold. In desperation Ruban ran to the corner store and phoned for an ambulance and Andy was rushed to the hospital.

For several days he was not allowed visitors. His friends were absolutely devastated, they couldn't understand why he suddenly passed out while speaking to someone through a slightly open door. They were told by the doctor that Andy had a concussion and they had no choice but to wait until they were allowed to speak to him. They nevertheless speculated in the meantime that perhaps a sudden shock resulted in his collapse.

"Something at the door must have surprised him," Ruben said.

"Like what? A ghost?" Bernie queried.

"We must wait for the answer until he can tell us," Ruben replied.

His friends sat at his bedside, waiting for Andy to show some sign of recognition, but his face remained blank. His eyes were wide open most of the time, staring at the ceiling. One day Bernie took his hand and spoke softly to him. "Andy, please look at me, tell me what happened the other day?"

Andy turned his head a bit, looked at Bernie intently; then, as though new life had come to him, he murmured, "The lady peeping out the door the other day was so much like Esther! Even though I couldn't see her in full view, that face floored me!" He licked his parched lips, rested a while, and continued, "Her profile was identical to Esther's. I only wish that I could have had a better look at her before she slammed the door in my face, and the world went into a spin. I don't remember a thing after that. Maybe there is something worth investigating?"

He took a deep breath and closed his eyes.

Bernie glanced at Ruben and both shrugged their shoulders in disbelief. "He must be hallucinating," Ruben quietly remarked. In the hotel room that evening, in a state of anxiety and bewilderment, they debated what they should do.

A few days later, they decided to go back to that house, hoping they might see the same woman again. Ruben knocked on the door and a woman appeared.

"What can I do for you?" she politely inquired.

"We have talked to a woman who was living here a few days ago and would like to speak to her again if possible."

Her eyes opened wide, then, in a sharp, suspicious tone of voice, replied, "The house was vacant when I moved in and I haven't seen anyone here since. I'm afraid there must be some mistake," and she closed the door in Ruben's face.

"What do you make of this?" Ruben commented to Bernie as they left the house.

"I don't know," Bernie replied. "It's beginning to sound like a mystery movie. She was here. We saw her. And for some unknown reason, she vanished."

After two weeks in the hospital, Andy was brought back to Bernie's house to recuperate. His health made slow and steady progress till he was allowed by his doctor to go out in a wheelchair. He would sit by the pool for hours and sometimes, he would think about Esther.

He remembered the day he and Esther arrived in Montreal. They rented a room above a store. It felt homey. They were happy because they were accustomed to that type of life in Winnipeg. The following day they made arrangements with a Rabbi to perform the wedding ceremony in his house. He remembered consoling Esther, saying, "My dear, to me you are the most beautiful girl in the world, and will be the loveliest bride even in an ordinary dress instead of the traditional wedding gown." He remembered kissing her tenderly after the ceremony and they cried on each other's shoulders, happy to have achieved the once impossible dream.

As soon as he was able to walk unaided, Andy made his way back to the house, hoping that he might be luckier. He knocked on the door. A woman responded immediately. She opened the door. "Yes, can I help you?" she asked, in a patronizing tone.

He briefly told her about his experience at this door several weeks ago and added, "I would very much appreciate it if you would permit me to come in for a few minutes."

"Are you by chance a friend of the two gentlemen who were here to see me some time ago?"

That question puzzled Andy.

"I don't really know about anyone who would have bothered you," he said.

"The men didn't bother me", the woman said. "I just didn't know what they were talking about, and I wouldn't let them in. I can understand your story and I think I know why you are here. So come in and sit down. You can tell me more about it inside."

She ushered Andy into a shabby living room, bearing visible scars of neglect. The walls and ceiling were a dingy gray, faded and blotchy with the passage of time. The bare floors were dark, brown, the colour deepened perhaps by an accumulation of ground-in dirt. There were a couple of well-worn upholstered chairs and a battered oak table on which were piles of old magazines and tattered books.

The woman pointed to one of the chairs and said, "Please sit down, Mr....?"

"Posarek, Andy Posarek", he replied. "May I know your name?"

"Just call me Jean — it's an easy name to remember. Make yourself comfortable. I'm going to make us some coffee. I'd like a cup, and you might too."

As Andy voiced his agreement, Jean left the room for what was presumably the kitchen. He turned to the stack of books and magazines on the table. He picked up a magazine, glanced at it and found nothing in it that appealed to him. He picked up another and in a casual glance decided that it too was of no interest to him. Perhaps the books might be better, Andy thought. The first couple he looked at were cowboy romances, which he promptly discarded.

He was about to give up his search for reading matter and to think again about what he should ask his hostess. But some power that was not his, that was beyond him caused him to try once more. From the pile he extracted a well-worn book, bound in reddish cloth. He glanced at the title — it was a novel, a mystery story by Agatha Christie. He was an Agatha Christie fan, and of course he had read the one he held in his hand. He was about to return it to the pile of books when it came to him. He remembered now. When they were in Montreal, he had bought that Agatha Christie mystery, bound in the same shade of red, and he had given it to Esther.

As he turned from the table, the book slipped from his fingers

159

and, as it fell, a much-folded, faded sheet of paper dropped from within its pages. He picked up the paper from the floor. By the way it was folded, he could make out some of the writing — it reminded him of Esther's. He read again the few words that he could see, "I forever will remember how genuinely you loved me". His heart began to pound, the sound reverberating through his ears.

Yes, within a few seconds he knew that he was looking at the handwriting of his long lost wife, he screamed with anguish, "It's Esther's, it's Esther's," and fell to the floor.

Jean ran from the kitchen, finding her guest had fainted, she fetched a glass of water which she poured over his head. With a pillow under his head, she tried to revive him. After a while, Andy, with Jean's help, sat up, clutching the paper in his hand.

He apologetically looked at Jean and murmured "I'm sorry, I don't know what came over me that made me pass out!"

Jean pointed to the sheet of paper and asked, "What is this you're holding in your hand?"

Only then did he realize the reason for his sudden fainting spell. He straightened out the paper and a bewildered, almost unbelieving look appeared in his eyes. The page read:

"Dear Andy:

Pray to God for me. Each time you pray remember to mention my name, say, 'God protect Esther, heal her wounded heart and soul, that she may have courage and strength to endure her agonizing life,' and I'll do the same for you. I left you my most precious possession — a bracelet to remember me by which was given to me by my mother when I was a very young girl. This bracelet was a gift to my mother from my grandmother when she was leaving for Canada. There may come a day when you'll have written me off as dead, and discard my memory out of your life as my parents did. In a way, they were right, I have been dead since I abandoned you. I prayed every day that you should find me, for I didn't possess enough strength to search for you. God knows I wanted to, and yet, I was hoping at the same time that you would forget me after a few years. I know I have inflicted horrible pain and sorrow upon you, because I forever will remember how genuinely you loved me. My life has turned into a frightening nightmare and I'm sorry for both of us. We wasted the most precious things we both had, love youth, and happiness.

Due to my Chassidic upbringing, however, and my stupidity, I found it increasingly difficult to adjust to a different way of life which at one time I thought would be easy. My father's orthodoxy and fanaticism through the years apparently influenced me and saturated my thinking more than I realized, and the last unforgettable emotional argument in the attic was constantly clawing at my brain and eroded my senses. For ten years I tried to make you happy, hoping that in time I would free myself from the guilt my father managed to infuse into my conscience, but I failed. If I only knew where you were I would mail this letter to you. This confession would be of some consolation to both of us.

Remember, my dear Andy, I have never stopped loving you.

Esther"

It was obvious by the old crumpled discoloured paper that the letter had been written many years ago.

Rather than relate to Jean the story of his life and the sorrow with which he had been living for the last three decades, he handed her the paper. "Here, Jean, read this. It will explain everything."

While Andy sat in silence broken only the by sound of a dripping water faucet in the nearby kitchen, Jean read the letter that had never been mailed. She handed the paper to him and asked, an obvious note of sympathy in her voice, "Have you ever given up hope of finding her?" to which he firmly responded, "No, never!"

Jean asked if she might read the letter again. After the second reading, she felt she had to tell Andy about a woman who had lived in the house and abandoned it recently.

"Maybe the owner of this house can help me!" he said, "Who owns it?"

The owner was a woman Jean told him and she lived nearby, just around the corner. "Her name is Clara Klein. Come, I'll introduce you to her."

Andy found in Mrs. Klein a charming, elderly woman of dignity and elegance. After hearing Andy's story and his somewhat vague description of the wife he had not seen for many years, Mrs. Klein reached for paper and pen, wrote an address, which she handed to Andy with the kindly words, "Here, try this, and good luck to you!"

Closely followed by Jean, Andy ran from the Klein house. He pulled up short when he suddenly realized that he didn't know Edmonton well enough to know the location to which Mrs. Klein had directed him. Fortunately Jean was still with him, and she guided him to an apartment house only a few blocks away. It was a rundown establishment — windows broken and cheaply mended, much worn linoleum on the hall floors which creaked at almost every step. The woodwork lacked paint or varnish. Andy's heart fell as he surveyed the forlorn interior, but he pressed on. With Jean helping him they knocked on every door. At the first half dozen there was no response. He kept on, until, on the third floor, there was an answer to his knock.

It was apartment No. 13 and Andy, although no more superstitious than the average person, wondered whether or not he might have better luck by skipping this one. By the time that thought entered his mind, he had rapped a couple of times at the door. It slowly opened inward on squeaking hinges and a face appeared in the narrow opening. It was a woman. She stared at Andy with frightened, bulging, glassy eyes, as though she could not believe she saw what she did. Her suffering face was deeply lined with wrinkles of suffering and her hair was completely white.

For a few agonizing seconds the woman clung to the door. She looked as though she was trying to say something but could not get the words out. Before Andy could say or do anything, her legs gave way and the woman slipped to the floor.

At almost the first look at the near-apparition that had appeared in the gloom of the opening doorway, Andy was sure he attained the goal he had set for himself many years before. As he bent over the woman who had collapsed before him, he knew that she was indeed his Esther. He put his arms around his beloved one and cried for help. He knew well what had happened, yet his mind had not yet grasped the enormity of the moment. His vision was blurred with tears he could not hold back and his senses were numb.

With Jean's help, they moved Esther inside the apartment and placed her on a dilapidated sofa in a dreary living room. She opened her eyes slowly, staring at the man kneeling beside her and clasping her hands in his. She said nothing, and closed her eyes again.

Although well aware now of what had happened, Andy could only believe it might be real by firmly gripping his wife's ice-cold hands. He did not dare move, lest the dream that had suddenly become a reality might just as suddenly burst before his eyes. He tried to speak, but he had lost his voice. At last he gathered all the courage he could muster and gently raised her hand and placed it against his cheek. A slight quiver shook her frail body, then she gradually relaxed. He spoke softly, directly into her ear:

"Esther, do you know who this is? Do you remember me?"

She looked at him for a few seconds, while her stare gradually softened, then wrapped her thin arms around his neck, and in a low voice he could hardly hear said, "You never should have found me. I don't deserve you after the horrible things I have done to you. I've thought about you every minute of every day, and I have died every time!"

Esther lapsed into silence, and Andy said nothing in reply. How long they remained like that neither could ever recall, nor did they care. It was only when Jean tapped him gently on the shoulder that Andy realized his dream was real and that he was indeed alive. He looked out the window and discovered that night had come. "It's dark outside", he said.

"But you're with me now and I don't care about the night", said Esther.

Covering her face with her hands, she cried and cried — the

163

flood gates had finally opened. Andy joined her in tears. They wept together until their tears at last washed away the anguish of their reunion. Late in the evening they were both in control of their emotions, the worst of the pain that resulted from their sudden meeting was over, and they talked eagerly together.

Jean slipped away to her home and left the reunited husband and wife to their reminiscences, which went far into the night. Andy mentioned the help Bernie had given him in the search for her.

"Bernie? My brother?" she asked. "Is he here?"

Andy told her that Bernie was not far from Edmonton; in fact, he was on a farm only a few miles away. He also told his wife about Rachel and the paralysis that had stricken her and about the loss of Michael, the son of so much talent and promise. Andy also said that as soon as she was feeling up to it he would take her to the farm for a reunion with Bernie.

"Oh, my God!" Esther cried. "How can I face him and live after what I have done to you and to him?"

Andy assured her of Bernie's understanding and that she need not worry about how she would be greeted. "Don't you fret", he said. "Bernie has always been on your side. And Ruben will be there, too. You must remember him!"

"Of course I do! How could I possibly forget such a dear friend?"

Andy made sure his wife was comfortable for the night, then made his way to the hotel, after assuring her that he would return early the next morning to help her get ready for the short trip to Bernie's. After the reunion with her brother, he told Esther, they would live together as they did so many years ago.

The meeting with Bernie was a tearful, yet happy, occasion. Even Rachel, unable to communicate, seemed to know, by a new look in her usually vacant eyes, what had happened and was joining in the celebration in the only way she could. Ruben welcomed Esther back to the circle of old friends and Brigette did all that she could to ensure that Bernie's sister was well taken care of. Bernie insisted that Esther and Andy stay with him as long as was necessary for the restoration of his sister to good health, mental and physical.

She questioned Bernie about his life since she left Andy and the home in Montreal. He told her of the loss of their parents, of his own joy in the marriage to Rachel, the pride he had had in the development of Michael in music, and then the disasters that had ensued in later years.

"I guess God was testing me to see if I could survive", he said with a trace of a smile, "and I did."

Bernie also told her of the remarkable way in which he had met Ruben in Winnipeg after many years of separation. "Nobody can understand the irony of fate", he said. "We all parted under most unusual circumstances and we were reunited by an invisible guiding hand."

There was little Esther had to tell about her life since she walked away from her Montreal home. She had moved from place to place through the years, never finding a spot that would ease her anguish over what she had done. She had finally chosen to live in Edmonton and found herself, as always, living among strangers in agonizing loneliness, not daring to hope that her situation would ever change. She frankly confessed that there was no one to blame but herself for the destruction of her own and Andy's lives.

Eventually Esther came to terms with her disturbed thinking. She accepted the consequences she had so mercilessly created and lived the best way she could, taking for her livelihood the humble jobs that were within her capacity to handle. In recent times she had turned into a recluse, barely existing on the modest welfare allowance that came to her each month. For years she wrote letters to Andy, yet never mailed them. She disposed of them in trash containers — all except one, that escaped the waste bin because she had folded it up and used it as a bookmark. Happily for both her and Andy, that was the book he had found.

Esther cleared up one minor mystery: the woman Ruben thought he saw in Bernie's old rooming house. When she had heard a knock at the door, she had opened it just enough to see that it was a man on the verandah. A sudden thought flashed through her mind: "If I didn't know better, I'd swear that it was Andy!" She quickly closed and locked the door, ran to the kitchen, where she squeezed into a broom closet and hid until she felt sure the man had gone. As soon as she could find another place, Esther moved away. Now she was filled with gratitude for the fact that Andy's determination had led to the fateful encounter at the door of No. 13.

With Andy and Esther reunited and Rachel showing slow signs of improvement, life was steadily, though gradually, returning to some degree of normality in the Appleman and Posarek families. Bernie, whose head had been bowed with sorrow for years, showed signs of regeneration. Rachel was gaining strength and showing signs of an awareness of events that had not hitherto mattered to her. With the help of a physiotherapist, Rachel slowly, little by little each day, was walking again. Some evenings she even joined the others in the living room. The gloom and the helplessness that had for so long overwhelmed her began to diminish and the long dulled eyes began to regain some of the sparkle that had been extinguished so long ago. It was a time of rejoicing for everyone.

Ruben was as happy as Andy and Bernie at the joyous turn of events. He was happy for them, for the restoration of Esther and Rachel to them, and for himself, with Brigette.

The time had come for the visitors to return to Winnipeg. That did not appeal to Ruben, who learned to enjoy life on a farm: the sun-drenched fields, the perfume of clover, the cows and the horses, the chickens, the family cat, and the birds that were everywhere. "It's just too good to last, I suppose", he muttered to himself. Then an idea came into his mind, a plan that, if carried out, would turn everyone's life around and make them all live happily ever after — if that were possible in this life.

CHAPTER 20

Alone with his thoughts, Ruben sat by the side of the pool, revelling in the warmth of the sunshine that had finally ended the days of rain. Ruben enjoyed rainy days, wet grass, soggy mud roads, and roadside puddles. They made him feel like a child again. On his father's farm, he had fun running barefoot in the rain and digging his toes into the mud.

But one can have too much of a good thing, and Ruben was content to see the storm clouds give way to blue skies, under which he pondered his own future and that of his good friends. His thoughts were interrupted by a cheerful-looking Bernie, who called out, as he walked from the house, "You seem to be deep in thought. Anything bothering you? Aren't you feeling well?" Bernie sat down and looked hard at Ruben.

"Not well, you ask? On the contrary, I never felt better. But I've been doing a lot of thinking since I came here and it has changed me a lot. I feel great and there's new meaning in my life."

"I'm really glad to know that and to hear that being at my place has helped you", said Bernie. "Now I have some news for you."

"About Rachel? I knew you were taking her to the doctor in the city but we haven't had a chance to talk since you got back."

Bernie was filled with happy excitement as he told Ruben about Rachel.

"I don't know how or where to begin, the news is so good. The doctor was absolutely amazed at how well she has got on in the past few weeks. It's been years since she showed any signs of improvement. Now there's hope that she's on the road to recovery

— I should say, to a limited recovery. The doctor asked if I could think of any one thing that had happened in the immediate past that might have been a contributing factor in her limited recovery. I could only attribute this miracle to Andy's finding of Esther and the reunion of all of us. I feel sure that these sparked in her an interest in living. She is surrounded now by loyal friends and family. She loves them and she feels loved by them. There's no other explanation that would make any sense."

Ruben agreed with Bernie that Bernie's interpretation of the recent events and their effect on Rachel made sense and he spoke words of warm praise for the years of care that Bernie had given his paralyzed wife. Then Ruben told Bernie what was uppermost in his mind:

"For some time, Bernie, I've been thinking hard about an idea that's now become a plan I would like you to think about, because you are very much involved in it." Bernie looked puzzled, and Ruben hastened to get his idea into the open.

"I've been at your farm and enjoyed your wonderful hospitality on two occasions now. During my stay here I have come to like rural life, I got very much attached to the way you really enjoy living. It's a grand place! Now here's the idea I have. I want you to consider it seriously.

"If I were to ask you to allow me to build a home next to your guest house for me and Brigette, what would you say? If my proposal doesn't totally meet with your approval, please, Bernie, tell me in simple terms, yes or no?"

"My dear Ruben, have you by chance been reading my mind? I have been thinking of the same thing. We would all share the happiness by living next door to each other, but knowing your city life style, I hesitated to suggest it to you!"

"How about Andy and Esther?" Ruben asked.

"I haven't approached them yet: I first wanted to hear your reaction. I am sure they would be only too happy to live here. We once lost each other. Let's not take a chance of repeating it again."

Ruben embraced his friend and noticed tears rolling down his face. Then they returned to the house to tell the others about their plan.

Ten months later, Ruben and Brigette were sitting on the balcony of their new freshly-painted house. Ruben opened a bottle of champagne, embraced Brigette, and asked, "Are you happy?"

"If I were any happier, I would probably burst. My heart is jumping and my senses somehow just can't comprehend that this is real. It's like a dream! It's crazy! I am afraid that I'll wake up any minute and the dream will be gone!" she whispered.

"Don't worry my dear, this is real, for good, for ever."

"I wonder what ever happened to Ingi?" she sighed.

"Please darling, don't think of him; he has gone back to where he'll be free and resume the kind of life he has been accustomed to!"

"Thank you, Ruben. I mean for everything. We are home at last!"

Andy and Esther, now together in the guest house, were trying to leave behind a lifetime of despair by picking up the pieces of the moment, adjusting, knowing and believing that at long last they had found each other.

Andy sat down on the sofa beside her, embraced her tenderly and said softly. "Esther, you know as well as I do that the past is beyond recapturing. The years have passed us by, but at the end we came out victorious. We have each other, and again we are together and nothing but death will separate us. Be happy with the way things turned out, and grateful to our friends and your brother for making this reunion possible. We will never part again. From now on until the end of time ....."

She put a finger to his lips and remarked, "Does end of time really matter?"

"Well," Andy replied, "let's live a day at a time, in happiness and contentment. The past is no more, the present is most satisfying. The future? We will let it take care of itself." He cupped her face gently with his hands and continued, "I'm touching you, I'm looking at your face, I'm kissing you, and yet, it all seems like a mirage that'll disappear with the blink of an eye. I'm sure though that this feeling is temporary. It's only a subconscious reaction to a lonely life of pain, sorrow and uncertainty. You have the face of an angel and the grace of a butterfly. I prayed for this day for countless years, let's not waste a moment of it!"

"How can you say that I'm beautiful when I feel so ugly!" Esther wanted to know.

"In my eyes you are the most beautiful woman I have ever seen."

He quickly changed the subject: "I very much appreciate your brother's kindness for inviting us to live in his guest house," Andy remarked. She cuddled up to him and whispered, "He is my brother and your best friend since childhood. Remember?"

Andy was quick to respond. "I certainly do, how could I ever forget it?"

That evening they celebrated the incredible miracles and twist of fate that brought them all together again. They were drinking, talking and joking about many insignificant but memorable episodes that had transpired over the decades.

"We were separated by uncontrollable circumstances and reunited by fate," Ruben said. "We should be called 'the brave and the restless'."

"We certainly had to be restless and brave in order to survive," Bernie agreed.

"I'll drink to that!" Andy replied, raising his glass.

Bernie embraced his wife with one hand and Brigette with the other. Ruben came over and warned him, "Handle with care, she is my girl and I love her!" He handed Brigette a glass of champagne. She looked at him lovingly even gratefully, and announced,

"You know, it's always been my ambition some day to be rich enough to eat with my fingers and sneeze out loud when champagne was tickling my nose!"

They all stood up, touched glasses and exclaimed in unison, "To tonight, to tomorrow, and to many years of happiness that will follow".

"Do you realize, it's two o'clock in the morning?" Bernie said after the toast. "How time flies when you're enjoying a special evening such as this with your dearest friends." They bade each other good night and separated.

In the guest house Andy and Esther sat in their living room without turning on the lights. Conversation was unnecessary, each knew what the other was thinking. The sky was very high, pale blue, studded with millions of sparkling stars; the full moon cast shadows on the walls. They were oblivious to time and sat together not uttering a word.

With the approach of dawn the sky at the rim of the eastern horizon slowly turned pink; the stars disappeared and the moon slowly dissolved.

"Let us take advantage of the moment and swear before all these heavenly bodies that we shall stay united and protect each other until the end of time," Andy said, while his eyes were getting moist.

"I swear", Esther replied. "Let's make up for some of the sad, lonely and wasted years."

They embraced each other and arm in arm walked into their bedroom and softly closed the door.

In their new house, next door, Brigette hung on to Ruben's arm, purring like a contented kitten. He embraced her, kissed her gently and said, "You go to bed, my dear. It's been a very tiring time for all of us, and I shall join you a little later." She went into the bedroom, leaving Ruben alone on the balcony.

Ruben stretched out on a chaise longue, focused his eyes on the glowing horizon and reflected on his life. It had all begun on that sunny spring morning when his brother Milty was killed. That tragedy had turned everybody's life around. He thought about the many people who had touched his life through the years. He visualized his father in Winnipeg, who on Fridays would be transformed from a button-hole maker into an angelic saint. But Ruben was too young then to comprehend the significance of his father's feelings.

Ruben became an agnostic, mainly to get even with the world by rejecting religion.

"How about Laura?" he thought. "She was a noble soul. I shall forever be grateful to her. She was a saint. Had she not helped me when I arrived in Vancouver I might not have met Helga, who was responsible for everything I have achieved through the years. I now thank God for giving me the wisdom to accept Helga's proposition at a time when I was totally helpless."

A smile crossed his lips. "Here I go again," he thought, "I am thinking about God once more." It's a natural reaction to a mellowed mind, he supposed. Considering the sequence of recent events, everything was possible.

For over forty years Ruben had tried to rebel against religion, but he had failed to divorce himself entirely from feeling and thinking about the traditions to which he had been exposed in his childhood.

As his eyelids became heavy with fatigue, Ruben slowly, but willingly, surrendered to a feeling of serenity, a feeling he had never experienced before in his entire life. As he drifted into this marvellous sense of peace, Ruben was content with the course of recent events. He was reunited with all his friends, in a way which even he, the non-believer, now looked upon as miraculous.

"All's well that ends well", he said to himself. "A winner never quits and a quitter never wins."

Later that morning Brigette found Ruben asleep on the balcony. She looked at him fondly and whispered to herself, "Thank God! We are all together, liberated, happy and content with our life. We have found an earthly paradise!"